T0078011

WHO'S WATCHING

TELENA D.

authorHOUSE®

AuthorHouse™
1663 Liberty Drive
Bloomington, IN 47403
www.authorhouse.com
Phone: 833-262-8899

Published by AuthorHouse 06/09/2022

ISBN: 978-1-6655-6002-3 (sc)
ISBN: 978-1-6655-6003-0 (e)

Library of Congress Control Number: 2022909189

Print information available on the last page.

Any people depicted in stock imagery provided by Getty Images are models,
and such images are being used for illustrative purposes only.
Certain stock imagery © Getty Images.

This book is printed on acid-free paper.

Because of the dynamic nature of the Internet, any web addresses or links contained in
this book may have changed since publication and may no longer be valid. The views
expressed in this work are solely those of the author and do not necessarily reflect the
views of the publisher, and the publisher hereby disclaims any responsibility for them.

Contents

DEDICATION

First I'd like to Thank God for blessing me to be who he created me to be. Without him there is no me and with Faith all things are possible.

This Book is Dedicated to My late Mother "Martha" and My Uncle Bill.

These two stayed on me about what was taking me so long to finish this book. So I took a chance and completed what they have always known that I could.

I also want to acknowledge my husband Damien for being the ear of my many Ideas and dreams for this book. (I Love you baby}.

Thanks to my Four Children Denquarius, Tiara, Telea and Tenea for their support and encouragement to continue. You all make my Heart complete!

A BIG Shout out to my Bestie (Chawana) for the challenge and bringing the idea for me to write.

To all of my family and friends who believed in me that I could do this. Thank you.

To my Readers Thank you for giving me a chance to get into your mind, and take you away from your normal thought process.

"One Step Forward is all it takes"- Telena D.

Chapter 1

During a hot shower, I begin to think about every sexual thought that possibly exists in the human mind. Like how I need a Man to kiss me from Neck to Knee and everything in between. How I wanted somebody to fuck me real hard, long and good. A long fat chocolate covered dick all the way up in me past my stomach. Anyway, thinking about all this shit, I felt my body temp rise; knowing that this feeling that I'm having is because it has been a long time since I've felt the touch of a man. I just can't imagine how my body will react to such Pleasure. Will I pass out from the contractions my body will give knowing that I can cum from someone other than myself. Will I, you know what, never mind, as I lather my favorite Caress Soap. I washed my body slowly not realizing that I was still making me feel good just from my own massage. Then my mind drifted again. This feeling of my pulsating clit and hard nipples is outstanding and I want me so bad but I must stop myself. No not here in the shower, as I began to think of all the things I wanted to do to this thick sexy ass body of mine. I closed my legs as tight as I could squeeze them to let the upper thigh muscles flex on each side of my clit "mmm that feels good" while watching my beautiful soaped up body in the mirror. Then my hand gently glided over my nipples and down to the hottest part of my body, "my juice box" as the rapper Gorilla Zoe calls it. I started to rub my clit back and forward enjoying the warmth of the water running over it as I was about to take myself to my highest peak and then once again I snapped back to reality. I barely finished the shower but I did and went ahead and got out and dried off quickly. I already had my clothes, shea butter, and Mango Butter oil from Hunnee Bz's store lying on my bed. I moisturize my body all over, then gently add the Mango Butter to sweeten the air. I put on my favorite Black t-shirt that says Stacked with a full figured woman on front and a pair of red silky thongs that I got off line. Since I'm kind of secretive about my lingerie I love shopping online that way no one can see the freak that buys the freakiest little pieces of nothing that I love wearing. I walked out of the bedroom, into the living room and I walked over to the patio doors and opened the curtains very wide.

I looked out at the Nashville Skyline and down at the river which is so relaxing. I live on the 15th floor and you can say almost Penthouse status, only because the Penthouses are right over me. Thinking to myself *yes girl you did all of this* and because of my success it makes my ego Big. I Quickly walked over to my bar and I fixed myself a shot of tequila and shot it fast and then poured another one to try and keep my mind off of me. Not thinking about the fact that Liquor turns me on like an Air Frying oven. Thinking *how petty of me, that I'm my number one fan though,* "damn I'm good." Passing the stereo, I decided to put on a little Isley Brothers; "Footsteps in the dark", now that's music for the soul. I slowly begin to rock my hips back and forward to the beat. I feel so sexy right now, I turned up the second shot of tequila and licked the rim of the glass. I danced so sexy watching the full figure me in the glass door, until the song faded into silence. The next song that came on was none other than the great Al Green, telling me;" don't look so sad," you know the song. "For the good times", oh I'm really feeling this one so I dimmed the lights and allowed my hands to feel freely all over my body. Singing "Lay your head…..on my pillow". I slowly slid open the patio doors, feeling so free and bold. Ready to take on anything that would cause me to lose control of the inter me. The night air was just right, not too hot or too cool and I wanted to seduce the air itself which blew ever so gently on my thighs causing a trip down memory lane when a man's touch was the reason for my sensitivity. I imagined only a room of gentlemen and I am the only woman, can you say center of all attention. I danced as if I could see all the men begin to get hard in their pants. I palmed my sweet pie slice as I began to apply deep pressure to my clit in circular motion. I damn near ripped off my shirt to run my tongue over both hard nipples. Normally I keep my dildo very close. It's just like my visa, I don't go anywhere without it. For the moment I decided to do something a little different. I grabbed my bullet from my purse and took it out on the balcony. I put it inside my thong and turned it to the lowest vibration just to feel the wetness around my firm clit. Then I moved the speed up to medium so I can get the rhythm and the sensation in unison. Lastly with the Bullet as high as it would go I felt my body take over in auto pilot. Moving faster and faster and shaking to the vibration as it stroked the top of my clit back and forward. I started to cum so hard I could feel the cramps in my stomach and thighs that wanted to attack my muscles because of how hard my body jerked. I left the bullet in place while my many clit-a-quakes continued to tremble. In the midst of all the satisfaction I was given myself with that bullet. I ignored the fact that my cell phone was ringing. Breathing heavily and refusing to go answer it I'll just let my voicemail get it. The phone stopped ringing but then started right back again so this time I moved the bullet from my very wet pussy and walked over to the bar where the phone was sitting. The phone had stopped ringing and as I was about to walk away from it, it rang again. The number was a weird one that I wasn't familiar with.

I answered on speaker phone figures it's just the wrong number. "hello" I say nonchalantly

A very deep voice speaks saying, "sexy lady this is WHO".

I said "excuse me, who would you like to speak to?"

He said" I'm WHO, who you need right now."

I said, "Who is this?"

"He says calmly my name is Who, the one who will suck those beautiful breasts, WHO will taste all your juices and WHO'S watching you right now."

I looked around and said oh shit. I dropped the phone on the counter not thinking he's still on the phone. I knocked over the bottle of tequila, glass and liquor went everywhere. I stepped on a piece of glass which was stuck in my damn foot while I ran and I cut off the lights, closed the sliding door and almost snatched my curtains down trying to shut them so fast. I never picked the damn phone back up. I just sit there scared, nervous, listening and looking around. The deep voice said "don't stop because of me…continue to satisfy my vision and release the cream that I crave." Using the light from the moon, I noticed a pair of flip flops over by the couch. I slipped them on so I wouldn't step on more glass and went and picked up the phone. I just held the phone first trying to control my breathing so he doesn't know I have it. Then he spoke very deeply, telling me that "he wanted to feel my breath on his chest once I allow him to take control of my shakes from the addition he will be bringing me." I yelled at him telling him that he has the wrong number and pushed the end button.

I got up and did a second check on my curtains and patio doors, made sure the door was bolted shut and then turned my lights back on. I was a nervous wreck. My thought to call the police was not clear enough to even figure out what I would say. I mean I could tell them what he was saying but they would have too many questions for me about what I was doing when I got the call, I just don't know what to do. I checked my cell to see if there was a block option and it's not so I'm going to have to install Mr. Numbers. This is one to jot down in the book. My pleasant night just turned Creepy and now I can't sleep. I went and cleaned the blood and mess I had made. I went to my closet and in my Jordan shoe box I got my 357-magnum aka (Jordan Black) fully loaded, my blanket, and my pillow. I curled up in my recliner for a long night of watching the damn door. What the hell is really going on??

Chapter 2

I pull up in the driveway with my lights off. I should have cut the car off and let it coast in the driveway, so his crazy ass can't hear me pull up. I get out of the car and close the door softly, taking my hip and bumping the door so that it closes without slamming. Even though I'm a grown ass woman, I'm creeping in the house like I'm still a teenager living at home with my momma.

I swear I hope this crazy bastard is asleep because if he isn't then shit about to hit the fan. As soon as I stuck that key in the door Carlos snatched it open and started yelling.

"Yea hoe, you thought I was asleep, didn't you?"

I said to Carlos, "I don't want to argue with you."

He replied with" Do I got stupid written on my face, what's the nigga name you fucking?"

I said "Carlos, you know I love you and what nigga you talking about? I' m not cheating on you baby, come on let's go to bed."

Carlos said "Bitch you got me fucked up, I give you everything you want and this is the thanks I get. You come in at 2:47 in the motherfucking morning all happy and shit. All yeah you are fucking somebody".

"Please Carlos, you are imagining things, let's not do this" headed into the bathroom."

"Tena get your ass over here to me right now and let me smell your pussy or else.

"Else what, Carlos? You're going to hit me? Huh? So I can continue to wear makeup to cover all the bruises. Does that make you feel like a man?" I said while taking off my earrings.

Carlos jumped up from the bed, with his gun in his hand and said, "bitch I said come here." I was so damn scared, I said in the sweetest voice my voice box could find "Please don't shoot me baby". I told him "do whatever you want but Please don't point that gun my way."

"Pull your pants down" he said and without hesitation I slowly pulled down my pants looking at him in his eyes silently asking why.

"Now lie down and open wide."

I did as I was told and then he opened my pussy and sniffed. Stuck in his finger and looked at it then tasted it.

With a trembling voice, I spoke softly "I feel so violated right now Carlos, you don't trust me?

"He got up and looked me in my eyes and said "this is my pussy, right?"

"Yes Carlos this is your pussy," as I watched him take off his boxers.

"If you ever give it away I will kill you Tena, do you understand me?"

"Yes Carlos; I understand" but really what I was thinking was *fuck you I been giving the pussy away and you can't even tell it dumb bastard.*

Then Carlos got down on his knees and started eating my pussy like it was the only pussy in the world. "Yes Tena this is all mine and I love it, it tastes so good."

Little did he know from 9:30 to 1:00 his boy Rico was tearing this pussy up. Carlos thinks I'm stupid I know he been cheating on me too, I just don't know with who. I swear one night he made me suck his dick and it smelled like ass, no not pussy, ASS you heard what I said. I can remember that's all he wanted from me at the beginning, he would say "he can't take no chances of me getting pregnant." For these last 6 or 7 months he never comes home on Thursday night. I don't say anything, So that's why I do what I do. I had to get over it, it wasn't easy at first but now who gives a fuck? Not Tena.

Anyways....See Rico is Carlos' main man and he supplies uncut cocaine to Carlos for a couple of thousand dollars cheaper than if he goes into Columbia and gets it himself. Long story short- Rico also used to go with Carlos' sister Caroline, but she died a year ago in a bad car accident. Caroline was 3 months pregnant with her first child. After the funeral Rico was so upset that he left and no one could find him for at least 2 months. We honestly thought he had killed himself or left the country.

I remember It like it was yesterday, early one Sunday morning last year in March Carlos had just left to handle some business in Texas. I was getting out of the shower and there Rico was standing there in the bathroom looking at me crying his eyes out. I grabbed the towel and put it around my body and went to Rico. I told him let me get dressed then we can talk about anything he wanted to cause I am here for you. Rico told me he just needed me to hold him, so I hugged him telling him that everything was going to be alright. Rico grabbed the towel and told me to make it right while kissing down my neck to my breast. I knew it was wrong but all my wild thoughts about him were coming true. Well yes, I fucked him right there in the bathroom. I rode him on the toilet; he bent me over the tub and the sink and fucked me so good I know I had about 6 orgasms. We showered together and fucked some more, went to sleep and fucked again. I should be ashamed of fucking this grieving man but I'm not. I am sorry about what happened to Caroline but it is what it is, and this is how the beginning of Rico and I started.

Anyways back to the story: I came good and hard with the fact that his boy had just got done Cumming all in this pussy, now Carlos is eating it up. Carlos told me to turn over while he continues to eat me from the back not to mention licking my ass. Carlos fucked my pussy like it was no tomorrow and then he decided that he wanted to fuck me in my ass tonight. Well I let him, I enjoyed it, I mean I loved it until we fell over in the bed tired from the wild fucking we had just done. I mean that I had done, I must admit I'm a soldier. Maybe because Carlos dick ain't the size of Rico is the real reason I can go again. It's amazing what a semi- frozen douche and mouthwash does for the pussy. So if I did get my ass whooped it would have been well worth it, Yes well worth it!

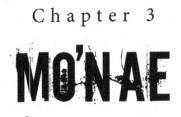

Chapter 3

Different day, but the same way of life you know work then home. I am so glad to get this week over and ready for the shutdown next week at work Since the President is quarantining the whole USA. *In need of a break* is all I can think about while getting off the elevator and walking down the long hall to my apartment. I came into the house, dropped everything, my purse and Lunch bag went in the chair. Keys were thrown on the table and kicked my shoes over by the closet. I couldn't wait to head straight to my fully loaded bar. Now out of the many Brandy's, Rums and Vodkas I have, I decided to pour a drink called Mellow Melody, introduced to me by my Aunt Liz and Uncle Jimmy a few years back. The drink consists of Lemonade, Orange juice and tequila; a sure guarantee to help you get true relaxation.

As I sit down to read my mail, I start thinking about how these last couple of weeks have been crazy but very interesting. Then my mind took over thinking about this man with the voice that called me and said that he was watching me. That was so weird, I mean who just calls someone and tells them some shit like he said and then that's just it. Crazy thing is the voice has a sexiness to it that affected me in many ways. I sit and I try to remember everything that happened that night, but the effect from the Mellow had done its job and before I knew it, I had fallen asleep. I woke back up at 10 o'clock p.m. on the dot, I got up and headed to my bedroom. I sat on my bed and laid-back thinking about the man with the voice. After about 5-10 minutes I got up and headed to the bathroom. I took a nice long hot bath and once I air dried and put on my oils I put on some red boy shorts and my black silk robe. I wrapped my hair and put my bonnet on.

As I was walking out of the bathroom, I felt my stomach growl. I forgot I drank alcohol and no food. So I went into the kitchen to fix a Bologna, mustard, and pickle sandwich. While getting the stuff for my sandwich, I heard the vibration from my cell notifying me that I had missed a call. I went over and picked it up and noticed that I missed 2 calls and had 2 voice mails. The first message was something about I won a free cruise, Delete with quickness. The 2nd one was the voice, I was so caught off guard by this message because it had been at least 2 weeks since I heard from him. I stopped doing everything, the pickles were on the table with no top, mustard was still in the refrigerator and the bologna was laying on the bread. The deep voice begins to speak as if I'm talking back.

He says "Red is my favorite color". I started thinking *did he see me put on these red boy shorts or is he still referring to the other week my red thongs.*

"Only a woman that hasn't been satisfied in a while would do the things that you do to yourself all these lonely nights". I looked at the phone like all these lonely nights and you don't know me sir.

He said, "let me be the one that fulfills all your fantasies". Now I'm thinking *how does he know about fantasies?*

Then he says, "Let me be your nightly medicine, freeing you from all pain and throbbing sensations". Oh shit, my clit just jumped real hard. I had to hold on to the counter to catch myself because my legs got weak. I could hear him breathing heavy as if he was pleasuring himself while saying:

"I would love to taste you while you're sleeping until your drips become streams". *This shit is turning me on, what in the hell is wrong with me?* The voice said" I will call you back when I think you're available." Just as quickly as he started talking it seemed like it ended even quicker. As bad as this may sound I didn't want him to stop talking, I wanted to hear more. I felt as if he could have made me cum, just listening to him.

I said to myself," mmm, mmm," shook my head and finished making my sandwich, put everything back up and then turned on the T.V. I watched a couple of episodes of Martin while eating my fancy bologna sandwich. I laughed too hard at this crazy ass Martin show, you know the episode when he fights with Tommy Hearns and gets his ass beat. As the show ended I got up to turn off the T.V and headed to bed, believe it or not the phone rang as if on cue. I answered it so fast, saying "Hello…he says "Hello sexy; I've been waiting to hear your voice." My breath became short and my heart beat sped up: "Who are you? "I asked.

He answered with, "I told you already, WHO; don't you, remember? "I told him, " Look, I'm getting ready to hang up the phone. `` I don't have time for these games, now who the hell are you?"

"Hey," he interrupted me… "haven't you ever wanted to do something over the edge, let me be that cliff? Balance yourself on top of me and I promise that I will not let you fall." Holding the phone listening, saying softly "I think you have the wrong number."

He responded with "I don't have the wrong number; you're the one that called me." Quickly I said, "Excuse me; I don't even know you."

He says" Baby, A few weeks back, while out on your balcony it was your body that called for me." I told him, "Look I haven't called you; I don't know you, please stop calling me." His voice got even sexier and he said:

"I'll stop for now but you don't have to stop." Now I'm confused" so I asked," I don't have to stop what?"

He said, "Calling for me in the night air, allowing your body's moister to make my mouth water and you're throbbing to be on the same beat as mine. When you're ready for me you know what to do, and he hung up the phone."

I was out done, here I sit with this dumb ass look on my face, thinking damn how somebody just gone call me and tell me what I need and want. As bad as I hate to say this he was right. Everything he said was the truth, but how did he know I never tell my business to no one. I was so surprised and yet so horny by this phone scene that just took place. I decided to make myself cum (in the dark) still thinking about this sexy ass deep voice. My thought of his appearance is a blank, I wish I could at least know something about him just to allow my imagination run free. At this moment, I wanted to fuck his voice, letting his everlasting Bass voice vibrate on my clit. When I tell you, I was fucking myself with my dildo thinking about this voice over the phone and as I began to think about some of the things he said to me, I begin to cum all over that dildo wishing that it was real and could cum back in me. After my heated sex scene with myself I cleaned up and went to sleep smiling thinking about all the what if's and hopes to dream about this voice all night.

Chapter 4

CALVIN

I have been waiting for this day for a long time and now it's here, Great Opportunities for me! I picked up my phone to call Kim, also known as the work snitch that keeps me informed on everything that I need to know. While waiting for her to pick up, I slipped on my shoes and grabbed my jacket. After about 30 seconds she answered "Good morning Calvin," 'I said Good morning Kim. Is there anything I need to know?" Kim went straight in talking, "somebody has been stealing lunches out of the refrig, knowing this Coronavirus is going on. Also Joe has been late everyday this week and I stopped her. "Kim, thanks I will take care of that and also have Mo'nae got to work yet?" Kims said "yes she's here, I think she is on an important phone call right now because she has a do not disturb sign on the door. Would you like for me to give her a message?" I replied "yes let her know I need to meet with her ASAP, I'm on my way, I'll see you soon." Kim said "Okay, I'll see you in a bit."

As soon as I hung up from Kim my phone rings again and it's my mom, I answered "Hello Mother.", "Hey baby just checking on you...do you gotta work today too?"... "Mom I've told you that I am the district manager over this Insurance Company so that means I have to work every day". Instantly mom said "Boy don't you get smart with me." I fixed that quickly. "Sorry Mom I'm not trying to be smart but I have to go over to the office on the North side today and

I like to leave early because of traffic." "Well since you are coming to my side of town you think you could bring some information about insurance for my neighbor Oscar. He doesn't have insurance and I told him you work for …What's the name of that company?" I said, "It's Living after Life mom…ok mom I gotta go"… "Calvin Lamont you bet not hang this Phone up she says angrily and what you got to come over this way for anyways?" "Mother, because the North side building is shutting down for a week or so for cleaning due to the virus that's going around. I have to make sure that the area manager gets her bonus and also give the other employees an extra week since we will be off." "Okay then baby, mommy loves you see you when you get here"… "Okay mom see you later, By Mom!" I'm beginning to worry about mom. I think she means well but she can be so mean at times. Even through her old mean ass ways, I will still honor thy mother. Anyways, I have to get on over to this office to see the beautiful Mo'nae.

I am so attracted to Mo'nae but she doesn't know it. I am going to ask her to go out with me. Now usually I don't go out with coworkers but it's something about Mo'nae that's a little different from other people. Mo'nae has it all. She is classy and sexy, I love to say her name sounds like something you can eat, hell maybe even drink. Something elegant so precious, her face and the thickness of her body longs for a man like me that will give her the world, take her places that she wants to go. I could make love to her in my mind over and over again. Her body is priceless. I'm scared that if I touch her I could contaminate her value and her soul. I wake up just to see her each day even when she doesn't see me. When I'm at the office and she is on break, I go into her office just to catch the smell of perfume she is wearing. Her caramel color and the way she keeps her hair fly makes me fantasize over her. She is the one that I want to walk into my dreams. If it takes me to not wake up to keep her there then let me sleep forever. She got everything she wants and needs, talking about INDEPENDENT (in my lil boosie voice) the only thing missing in her life is me. I want to be the one she's waiting for because it's her that has my heart and she doesn't even know it yet but she will, very soon. I have been checking her out for some time now. I watch her as she twists back and forward around that office, not taking mess from anybody. Mo'nae does her job and means business; always on a professional level and never putting up with no drama. I like the fact that she is bossy but yet so sweet at the same time. I never get any complaints about her, matter of fact everyone loves her. So do I but I love her in a way that does not exist by another soul, I invented this love well atleast I think I did. In order to get the same kind of love back I must do whatever it takes to get her to fall in love with me. Lots of people think it takes a long time to fall in love, but in reality when it's real love, you know it Right then and there. Can you say love at first sight? Yep there it is yes I said it. It does happen this way and for anyone that has ever experienced it then you know what I mean. I guess you are wondering how I know so much about her, it's because when you want to get an A in a subject you must study first…I'm on a mission to please!

Chapter 5

When I first walked in at my job it was like I was a new person. Everyone was saying good morning to me and smiling like never before. I got paranoid because this was something new and then I asked Kim "why is everybody so cheerful this morning?' Kim said 'because she heard from a little birdie that the company might be closing for a week or more for cleaning, and that she may have told a few people.' Even though I heard it too, I told her,'don't spread rumors if you're not sure if it's true or not.' Kim said okay sorry and walked off. Damn a week off, shit if I wasn't single I'd be laid up the whole week. Thanks to that ex-boy I used to know is the reason I'm single now.

See I used to have this boyfriend and yes I called him a boy because that's what he acted like. His name was Keith. He was very sexy, he stood about 5'10 thick and muscular because he was in shape and was always at the gym. Big nice arms that could handle a woman. Medium brown with slanted gray eyes, curly black hair and juicy lips that were made with a suction. Keith made me feel so good in bed and that tongue was long enough to lick my ovaries, well maybe I'm exaggerating a little but his tongue was long enough to do some great tricks with it. Keith would do almost everything I wanted him to but Keith was a dog and he deserved to have Scooby snacks for being a damn good DOG!

He had a great job for a little while working for the post office until this fool went to work high one day. I guess he didn't think no one noticed until his ass went back the next day and they tested that ass. Once they got the results back he was fired on the spot. Well this fool acted like he was going to work every day just as I was, until one day I had to run to the post office while on my break. I asked where he was and they said he doesn't work here anymore. I said what you mean he doesn't work here anymore and Joe the manager said he didn't tell you, we fired him a month ago.

Talking about a mad bitch, I was pissed the fuck off. I was on my way home when I saw him standing on the street corner with his little thug ass friends, and he was just leaning over in a car and was selling dope. I knew that he kept plenty of money those last few weeks but dope I never thought. I jumped out the car and said 'so this is what you doing; you want to jeopardize everything we got to sell fucking dope?' He walks over talking about 'let me explain.' I said 'explain on your way to the house to get your shit.' Speeding down the street, I called my job and told them I couldn't come back because of an emergency. When we got home, he told me how sorry he was and asked me please not to put him out. Keith told me that he loved me and he didn't want our relationship to just end. After a few tears and sorrow, I was a softy so I fucked him and made all the bad things go away for the moment, until there was a knock at the door.

Keith jumped up and said he would get it but I'm nosey so I eased out the bed and besides who would be knocking on the door this time of day if we both are supposed to be at work? He opened the door and a girl was standing there talking about 'you said I could come back today.' He said in a whisper, ' not today she is at home.' Loudly, I said' I'm sure in the hell am home and who are you?' With much attitude this little heifer said "I'm the one he told to come back today and get some more dick and who are you?" Keith said "this little bitch is lying" and tried to slam the door in her face. I pushed him to the side and I asked the girl how long they'd been messing around, she said for a couple of weeks. I told her thanks and to have a good day.

I shut the door, grabbed the trash can and went into the room.

Keith was behind me talking about don't believe that shit baby, don't do this. I started throwing his shit in that trash can and I told him to get the fuck out my house. "It's one thing to fuck a bitch, but fucking in my house I don't think so." I told him "you just threw 3 years of my life away I could have gotten someone else but no I chose your sorry ass." Me saying that made him mad and this fool ran up and hit me in the mouth saying that "I got him fucked up." No this mother fucker didn't saying to mself while running to my closet to get my pistol and shot at his ass 3 times, he was running, ducking and flipping, I missed but he knows not to fuck with me again. You know I never heard anything else from that fucker.

After that I went into a depression for a while; I never let anyone else in. Men would try and holler at me but I would just say that I was in a relationship, lying to them and myself just making the situation worse. During my depression I gained 50 pounds so I feel like no one has even noticed me since. It has been two years since I was in a relationship and since I had some dick. My body has a mind of its own lately. That's why I bought myself a toy to play with. Even though many of the night's I've wished for someone to give me what I want and need. Damn I sound like the unknown voice that called me last night. My mind drifted off, *I wondered what he's doing, no I don't I don't even know this person. Why did he call me? How does he know these things about me? Has he been watching me for a long time? Does he know my name? Does he work with me? He could possibly live in the same building as me. I don't have a clue who this person is. In a way I want to know, but then again I don't.*

"Mo'nae, -Hello," said Kim, who was just standing at my desk calling my name. "Dang girl," said Kim "who got your mind away from here, I have been calling your name for a minute" then in a whisper she said, "You Good?" *Damn I forgot I was at work, how long was I in this daze thinking about a man that really does not exist but really does at the same time.*

I looked at her and said "Yes honey I'm fine, I was just thinking about all the things I need to do when I get off work." Kim looked at me and said "Calvin called and said that he would be here soon and needed to meet with you ASAP." Then she said "maybe you should see if he's single." I said "Kim, my personal life isn't any of your business, and I would appreciate it if you wouldn't tell me what I need to do". I said "no, what you need to do is get back to work before you are sending out resumes tomorrow." Kim looked at me and said "excuse me for living. I was just kidding with you, you need to loosen up a little everybody isn't out to get you" and turned and walked out of my office. Oh I guess you know my brain went into panic mode. *What does she mean "out to get me", everyone is suspect now. Is this one of her little pranks with the voice? Maybe I'm just looking for someone to blame, because I don't know. Maybe I should tell someone just in case something happens to me, but who would actually believe this kind of nonsense exists?* I guess I'll get to work so I can look busy when Calvin comes for this meeting.

Chapter 6

TENA

"Damn Ri...Baby that feels so good,' saying while half asleep before I could open my eyes to see who was giving me the morning dick. Carlos punched me in my mouth.

"Bitch who did you just call me?"

"Nobody baby," then I said "let me up" while grabbing my mouth. I could feel the blood filling up in my mouth and my lip throbbing with much pain.

"You were going to call me somebody's name starting with an R, weren't you?"

"No I wasn't, I was getting ready to say it's really good, baby please let me up?"

"Hell no, you ain't going nowhere," then Carlos sat on my stomach and put his hands around my throat. He said "bitch I'm going to let you go this time but next time I'm going to break your fucking neck. Call me another motherfucker's name and see stupid bitch and then got off of me.

I ran in the bathroom to see what damage he had done to me. My lip was busted on the inside top and bottom. I felt like Tina Turner in the "What's love got to do with it" movie, you know the scene from after the limo. I sat on the side of the tub crying because I knew I had just fucked up and I am lucky to be alive. I cleaned myself up and left the bathroom.

Carlos was sitting on the bed looking at me like he was going to kill me for real. He told me to come to him, I was scared but I still went. "Suck my dick" he said with much hate in his voice.

"My lips are sore Carlos I can't."

He said, "I don't give a fuck, suck it now you petty Bitch." I did, I sucked his dick, and it hurt so badly that I wanted to bite the motherfucker off but I knew he would kill me for real if he even felt my teeth at the moment. Carlos came in my mouth and hit me in the face with a stack of 20's. "Here go fix yourself up" he said, "I got to go out of town later today. These 2000 dollars should make you forget about me punching you right?" He asks me "Who loves you baby?" "You do daddy" I said and he kissed me and left out the door.

I waited about 30 mins after he left, then I left and went to the bank to put the money in my private account that no one knows about under my real name (KaTena Wickson). I added the money with the other 90 grand that he had given me for ass whooping. No, I don't like getting beat but I'll be rich one day. Every time Carlos gets mad at me for something he always gives me at least a grand because he feels bad for hitting me or cursing me out whichever abuse he feels like for that day. It's all good because every time he beats me I go and do something that makes me feel good.

About an hour before I texted Rico to see if he was with Carlos. Twenty minutes later he texted back, saying that Carlos would only be dropping off a package then turning right back around heading home and that he would have to holler at me another time. I erased the messages and took a bath then I decided that right now is the best time to get a good nap before he got back home. Laying here thinking *if Carlos will do this to me and he thinks I'm cheating then what the hell will he do if he finds out I really am. Oh well by the time or if he ever finds out I'll be long gone.*

See I know that to everyone I am a fool for staying with his abusive ass. I do have a plan to get away from him and I know a lot of people that he knows. They tell me to leave him and they will take care of me. I don't want to fall back into this type of situation. I want to be able to start a family one day with the right man, hell I'm 32 and have lived this type of life since I was 18. Just wilding out for no reason at all. See I love money and sometimes you have to do what you have to do in order to get it. Call me what you want, if money is in it then I'm in it. Then in the end I will have everything I want without Carlos. For all the wrong he has done to me, his time is surely coming. Like they say Karma is a Bitch!!!

Chapter 7

I have been the area manager for this Insurance company for about 3 years. I have 25 wonderful employees that work under me and everyone seems to think that I'm mean, when in fact I'm really the opposite. I don't have to prove anything to anyone, I just believe that work is work and that's just the way it is. I don't mean to come off as a mean person, I just know when you start interacting with the co-workers on another level then that's when things start to go wrong, trust me I know this by experience. So to keep it right I just try to keep it on a professional level at all times. Since today is Friday and next week the whole company will be closed for Cleaning, I've decided to buy my employees lunch today. You should have seen the looks on their faces when I told them. They began to whisper and I just looked at them and smiled and told them to enjoy it. Whatever they wanted I paid for it this was my way of showing them that I appreciate the good work they have been doing. I turn to walk back in my office and in walks the district manager with his sexy ass. Mmm!

His name is Calvin Williams and handsome as fuck, bald head with a go-tee with streaks of gray in it but most of all his charming character was the best part. He knows how to speak to a lady and make me have nice thoughts about him. As from what I could see he has a nice body, he always smells great and that ring finger is empty.

Not that I'm keeping an eye on him but hey something that nice makes you wonder where in the hell is his woman.

Calvin walks in my office and asks if I have a second to chat, nervous because of all my thoughts about him I said yes sir and he came in. He told me that he came to the office because he knew that the company would be closed next week and he wanted to see how things were going before I left for the day. I told him that everything was good and that one of our best employee's Ms. Sarah, would be in to check on the office while it was closed. He knew that Ms. Sarah would make sure everything was alright and notify him if need be. Ms. Sarah was loyal and had been with the company for 20 years, her education wouldn't allow her to get a higher position; even though she had moved up 5 times already. It was nothing that she didn't know about the business, she was our go to person for lots of things, and a position was nothing to her because she owns some stock.

Calvin came straight out, did not hesitate and said "Mo'nae there is something I've been wanting to ask you." I said "sure go ahead" as if I wasn't anxious to know what he was about to ask me. He asks "how would you like to go to dinner with me?" I got choked up and couldn't believe that he asked me that. I was sure it was going to be something about this job but hell he just flipped the strip all the way around. Although, I had checked him out a few times because I think he is sexy as hell. Before I knew it, I kind of let out a quick giggle like a young school girl with a crush and then said "yes." I thought about it and said to myself *my brain needs to catch up with my mouth.* Calvin said "I didn't ask you to do anything else but have dinner with me". That's it, nothing else. I looked at him like what you mean nothing else, but I decided oh well what the hell. He told me he would pick me up at 7 tonight. Thinking *Wow he is moving quick Shiiiit…so am I?* I smiled and said that would be awesome, wrote down my number and address with quickness and handed it to him before he changed his mind. Sounds like I'm desperate don't it.

On his way out of my office he put his hand on his head and said "oh I almost forgot" and handed me an envelope and said "this is our appreciation to you for a job well done. He also stated that all employees would get a week's pay because of the shut down." He grabbed my hand, gave it a gentle kiss and left the office. I opened the envelope and out fell a BONUS check for $5000.00. I was speechless. I read the card that had all management signatures on it. I put the card and check in my purse and walked out to use the bathroom because that kiss on the hand made my panties wet, yes my mind went there...*Those soft lips on this coochie mm mm mmmmm.* As I walked out there stood Kim looking at me smiling and winked at me while shaking her head like she saw what just happened. For some strange reason her wicked smirk got on my nerves. I just shook her off and I went to the restroom. After peeing I wiped, I couldn't believe how wet I was just because he asked me on a date and a damn hand kiss. (Damn I guess that's just a little of the Freak in me seeping out). Once I walked back into my office there were a dozen roses and a card that said patiently waiting for a good night. Kim walked in and said "Mo'nae I brought them in, it was a secret that I knew about. Calvin always asks about you but"...I cut her off; "that's fine Kim Thanks for a well-kept secret, you can leave now. I have to get my things together so I can enjoy next week off. By the way Kim, you were right." Not sure if I care but Kim had a strange look on her face like she wanted to say something but instead she said "okay" and left. I went to my desk to admire the roses and I took one out and smelled it, and with the biggest smile leaned on my desk thinking about the night to come. Can you say Too Excited!!!!!

Chapter 8

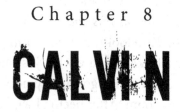

CALVIN

Super happy about later on I needed to take care of a few things before my big night. I headed over to my mom's to drop off this insurance information for Mr. Oscar. I started realizing something has got to be going on between my mom and that man because he is all she talks about. Oscar is always in need of something and it's so funny how mom is always the one he calls for it. I pulled up in the small parking lot because where mom lives is a high-rise for the elderly and not everyone has a car or can drive. When I got out of my car Ms. Neddie was sitting out front of the building meddling like always, she looked at me and licked her old ass tongue out at me like in her sexy way. "**Eww**" I said while turning my head so quickly until I almost gave myself whiplash.

I went in the building and I knocked on the door and it took awhile for her to open it so I pulled out my key to go in and just as I got that key in the door, Mom opened it; her wig and dress was a little twisted and he sat down real quick. I asked "was everything okay?" She said "yes", dimmed her eyes at me and asked me "what I was trying to insinuate?" I told her "nothing" and I straightened her wig up. Mom was embarrassed at the thought of me even thinking about what she and Oscar were possibly doing. Mr. Oscar's cool ass sitting there looking guilty and dropped his head and asked me "how was I?" I told him "great" in my sarcastic voice "now that I know my mama is into new things" then I smiled real BIG. Mom said "watch your mouth boy," I laughed again and said "okay sorry ma." I handed Mr. Oscar the insurance info and asked if he wanted me to explain it to him and he told me that he would read it later and if he had any questions he would let me know. Oscar told mom he would talk to her later and headed for the door. I reassured him that he didn't have to leave on my account. Mom jumped up, pushed my head and said "hush boy" as she walked him to the door and in a soft voice mom told Mr. Oscar to call her later, he said he would then he kissed her on her cheek, they giggled like teenagers as he walked out the door. Mom came back in there pointing her little finger in my face telling me "don't ever disrespect her company again," "But Ma!" "hush" mom said "I'll slap the b- lack off you." "Mom I was just kidding, can you tell me about you and Mr. Oscar, is that your Boo thang?" Mom said "what the hell is a boo thing?" "Not thing ma thang!" But seriously I know there is something and it has been going on for a long time. You don't have to hide anything from me, remember I'm just your son." Mom got excited and started saying, "well I do like him because he is such a gentleman and he always comes over and we watch TV shows together and I cook and he helps me, then he rubs my feet." "Hold on ma" I said, "too much information," "but if you like him that's cool I just want my mother to be happy so I approve of him." Mom got up and gave me a great big hug and said "that's so sweet of you son but with or without your approval he wasn't going to stop tapping this ass," while trying to give me dap. I almost puked all over her floor and told her she gets no dap from me. After all her laughing and she calmed herself down I told her I needed a few pointers and I told her about my date. Mom asked me who she was and I told her all about Monae. Mom said "son I want you to remember this one thing; think about the way you want Mr. Oscar to treat me and you have your answer." That was it, I didn't need any more advice because I love my mom and I know that no one bet not ever treat her wrong or disrespect her in any way. I got up and kissed my mom on the cheek and told her "that was the best advice ever, now I'm on my way to get the woman of my dreams." Mom said "call me and let me know how it goes," I told her I would and while leaving out the door I could have sworn I heard her say, "He's gone." Laughing to myself Oscar must be on speed dial. Don't you know before I even got out of the building the elevator opened up and Mr. Oscar was getting off headed down to mom's door. I got to my car only to find some old ass peppermint sticks on my windshield. I looked around at Ms. Neddie who was still in the same spot, she said to me "don't you want to see how I can put those sticks in my mouth?" I said "HELL NO," jumped in my car and burnt rubber getting the hell away from there.

Chapter 9

Honey, when I tell you Kim is something else, we used to be very close. We worked together at another Job about 7 years ago, before starting this one. We would go out to happy hour, talk lots of girl talk, and just do girl stuff like shop and gossip. Kim is what men call an Amazon type of gal you know, the ones with big ass and tits and tall as hell, not a single skinny bone in her body. Okay so one of those nights back then, me and her decided to go to this club named "Anything Goes" and trust me the name spoke for itself. There were girls on girls, men on men, men on girls, and then alcohol. That was enough to let me know I was ready to get my freak on and be as freaky as can be in the place. Kim and I were watching this couple fuck in a private room. Then the next thing I remember was she and I were going at it, kissing and touching and sucking on each other's tits. The couple was so into what we were doing until they stopped fucking just to join us. Kim got fucked by the husband and the wife ate both of us. When we finished with them we went home and enjoyed each other for two whole days. It was my first time and it was fun, Kim said it was also her first but I don't know because she was a professional pussy eater. A week or so went by and I decided that we wouldn't continue being together on that level. It was fun, something to try and something that I'm glad I experienced, really just another task off my bucket list. I think Kim wasn't really ready to stop, and then all of a sudden she just stopped talking to me for a while. Everything she had to say to me she kept it brief and kept her distance for almost a year. Then one day I was ready to bury the hatchet, so I invited her to my birthday party. Believe it or not, Kim was excited about me asking her to come and was more than willing to help me decorate and set up food. I told her that I was glad that she decided to come and I was glad to have her back as my chill buddy. The party went on and we partied till the break of dawn. When I finally did wake up my house was clean and everything was nice and neat and Kim was still there. She told me that she knew I was faded and couldn't do all that stuff by myself, so she stayed and made sure I was okay and cleaned up the mess everybody had made. So from that day on we have been back cool but I still worry about her a little because of the way she looks at me and just some of the things she says. I think she still wants me in a way because even though I can say all the freaky stuff we did, it still makes my Lily sprout every now and then. I often find Kim standing back in a corner watching me. No matter what I do, wear, or say, Kim always has a comment. I don't think she is a hater but she has a cocky type of style. I know she wants to taste this cookie again but she is going to learn that she can't have it her way this is not Burger King.

I can say this about Kim, she is one working ass sista who knows her job, never late and is on the come up in this place. I'm thinking about mentioning her name to my boss because really she needs her own office and team, that way she can stop spying on me I'm just saying. But in reality she is one hell of a worker and deserves to be rewarded for it. I'm going to have to pull her to the side and talk to her soon because I really want to know what's on her mind.

Chapter 10

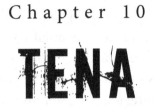

It had been a long time well maybe a week since Carlos last hit me, I am so sick of his shit that's why I cheat on him cause I'm not stupid I know he fucking other bitches too. Carlos had left to do some work for a friend of his, after about a couple of hours or so his brother Chris had stopped by to see him while on this side of town. Chris was fine as hell, bow legged with that smooth Columbian skin, 5'9 with deep dimples and pink juicy lips. I opened the door and he was like "dayum ma you looking good." I smiled as he walked past me, still sizing me up. Chris said "can I get a hug I am your brother in law." I told him "no, you're not my brother-in-law, I'm not married to no one." Chris said "stop that now because you know you are Carlos' #1." I know he said that shit to slick snitch on Carlos cheating motherfucking ass so just for that I gave Chris a hug with a little rub and he gave me much more. As we were hugging he started to squeeze on my ass. One of my weak spots but he didn't know it, well he does now because before I knew it, I was on the floor being fucked perfectly by my lover's brother.

The moment was so intense I didn't hear that someone else had come in, but I just felt more hands on my breast and something big on my mouth. I looked up and there was their uncle N.J with his dick on my mouth. N.J. wasn't an old uncle he was the one close to Carlos age, you know mother and grandmother pregnant at the same time type of shit. N.J stood for no justice, due to his recent stay in Kentucky's Federal Penitentiary. Locked up for 7 years for something he says he didn't do, but being a relative of Carlos I find that hard to believe. N.J. looked at me like I really didn't have a choice, so I went to sucking that big ass dick and looking at him in his eye like you bet not say a motherfucking word, and he was looking the opposite like you better suck this dick or else he was going to tell. While Chris fucked my pussy good and N.J. fucked my mouth good I started squirting all on Chris dick, N.J. heard it and it made him cum in my mouth. Chris yelled damn this shit feels good as he pushed his nut all in my pussy. We all were coming together, sounding like we were trying to find a tune, so we could audition for American Got Talent. After we finished, I told them that Carlos would be here soon and they should leave. N.J. said "no I'm going to chill and wait for him," Chris said "shit me too."

Chris looked at N.J and said "I'm not saying a word, I just paid Carlos ass back for the many times he did me." N.J. said "you too?" as they pounded each other's fist. I was a nervous wreck. I washed up, brushed my teeth, and even took a shit because I was so scared that they were going to tell Carlos when he got home.

As I came out of the bathroom Carlos was pulling up in the driveway. I guess they could tell that I was scared shitless that they told me to chill out and this was our little secret. I said "please don't say anything because he will kill us all." N.J. said "no doubt" and Chris said "my word is my bond." I felt a sigh of relief as I headed to the kitchen to get three beers. I met Carlos in the foyer, handed him a beer and gave N.J and Chris theirs too. Carlos told me to go wait in the room and that he needed to holla at his boys privately. I did not argue with that. I hurried my ass right in the room so I could listen through the vent to what they had to talk about.

I got in the room and sat down on the bed softly talking to myself. I just cannot believe I just fucked Chris and N.J. What is wrong with me? I act as if I have an addiction. Maybe I do, maybe I need help. I get so much pleasure just knowing that what I'm doing is so wrong. The fact of wanting to be caught I think makes me cum even harder.

I think I know why, because all the hurt and pain that Carlos has caused me, I want him to hurt just as much or even more. Carlos, he goes for my outsides with the bruises but I want to go for his insides like his mind and heart. I really think he loves me but he has a funny way of showing it. I don't have the same kind of love for him but hell the way he punches me, maybe there is no love on his part either. This kind of love/hate relationship never works, that's why I know I have to get away soon because someone will end up fucked up and I have no intention of it being me.

I heard Chris and N.P say "What" and then it got quiet. I got down by the vent and all I heard was Carlos saying "yea and there is a baby I need for y'all to make this go away." After that I heard the door open and close. I jumped up and sat back on the bed. As soon as I laid back, Carlos walked in and said "My dick hard, what are you gonna do about it?" I thought to myself, cut *the motherfucker off and what about a baby?* I said "whatever you want Daddy?" I guess you know I had to fuck him too, Shit my mouth and insides are tired yall.

Chapter 11

I have to figure out what kind of outfit to wear for tonight. I'm really looking forward to this because it's been such a long time since I went out and enjoyed myself. Once home I had to sit down for a second just to enjoy the silence. I went to the balcony and opened the door. I stepped out hoping to catch a glance of the person with the voice. I looked in every direction. I even looked up at the Penthouse over me to see if they could see me and there's no way anyone can see me not unless they live in the apartments a mile over and using binoculars, is that possible? Anyway, I know I need to start getting ready, so I ran my bath. I got out a pair of white cut up jeans from Fashion Nova, that fit really nice on my big round butt. I grabbed my favorite black low cut Michael Kors blouse that shows enough cleavage on these 44 double D's but not too much, you know classy not trashy and my new Black, Michael Kors stilettos.

Remember I am a BBW; I weigh 210 pounds and am thick with it. I am caramel colored with short hair that I keep fresh to death. I'm only 5'5, but that's ok, I'm not trying to please no one but Calvin for the night. Leave it to the professional to say that I'm overweight and I know it but right now it's not important. I hope that Calvin is impressed with the way I look and that he really wants to get to know me on a personal level. I mean I do look good at least I think so. If I can't compliment me then how am I supposed to hope the next person will. I'm so soft to the touch, and I'm all woman to the bone. "Yes I fit the description of a real woman seeking a real man that will make me feel real good Real quick!"

Okay my bath is ready, so I got in and relaxed. I'm really nervous because I haven't been out with a man in a long time and time seems to be flying. I'm sure tonight is going to be a great one because Calvin seems really nice but on the other hand I just don't want to be disappointed. I have been let down in the past by men that just wanted a quick nut and that wasn't about to happen, then or now. Well then again the man with the voice has me thinking twice.

In a blink of an eye it's 6:30 already, shit that was fast, so I finished putting lotion all over my body. While getting dressed I'm thinking will tonight move this fast or will it be slow? I guess I need to get out more because I'm so tired of this lonely life of mine. Oh yea I remember Calvin asking me about a perfume I was wearing one day, so I will put some of it on and maybe if he gets close enough he will remember that it's the one he asked about.

"Girl you know you look damn good" I say to myself while looking in the mirror.

At exactly 7 on the dot my phone rings, it's Calvin. He said he's down stairs waiting for me. I asked him to come up for a minute and he agreed. Oh wow, this will be the first man since Keith that I let come into my apartment. Of course I've had a party or two but never a man just coming to pick me up. I feel marvelous, beautiful, important and anxious as hell right about now. I finished putting on my makeup and did a last peep in the mirror. I was satisfied with the way I looked and smelled and so now I wait for the doorbell.

Chapter 12

CALVIN

I rang the doorbell and when Mo'nae opened that door I was amazed, looked her up and down and said you look wonderful, she dropped her head and blushed a little and said thank you. "You're very handsome yourself, come on in" she suggested. She said she had to grab her purse and she'd be ready, she asked me if I wanted a glass of wine before we left and I said sure. Mo'nae poured us a glass and we chatted a little about stuff until we were ready to go. I got up and asked, ``Are you ready?" She said "yes" then motioned for her to go out first so I could lock the door for her. She gave me the keys and watched as I made sure her place was secure. I held my arm out and she grabbed it as we walked toward the elevator. I pushed the down button and waited for it to open. On our way down I stared at her beauty and once she saw me through the mirror on the elevator door she just looked at me and smiled and was like what, is something wrong? I reassured her that nothing was wrong as she stepped out the elevator in front of me. I was trying my luck when I put my hand on her lower back as we walked toward my 2020 Tesla Model S. I opened the door for her, and watched her as she sat down so softly in the passenger seat. I got in and started the car. "What kind of music do you like?" I asked. Mo'nae answered "anything slow or old school." I turned on Luther Vandross greatest hits and We headed for our place of destiny and enjoyed each other's conversation on the way. I told her how beautiful she looked and once again she blushed and said "Thanks." Mo'nae asked if I was going to compliment her all night. I told her I really had a reason too because she was just that fine. Mo'nae said will you stop it while laughing. I laughed and said ok for now I will quit but you will want me to later.

We arrived at a new 5 star restaurant named "Steak Palace". We valet parked and I took her by the hand and led her into the building. I had made reservations for us already; I knew what I wanted and what to do to get it. We were seated and got our drink of choice. The waitress asked "what were we having to drink?" I ordered a Courvoisier on the rocks, she ordered a shot of Patron 1800 with salt and lime and ordered a margarita on the rocks still made with the top shelf. I asked her if she was sure she could handle all that because I didn't want her to get torn down before the food. Mo'nae expressed that she just wanted to knock the edge off a little.

I guess 10 minutes passed before the waitress came back with our drinks and took our food order. As soon as the waitress walked off Mo'nae first licked the back of the glass, then downed that shot of patron and sucked the lime. Monae looked at me and said, "In a few minutes I will feel a little better, I got my courage juice." I told her she was a No limit True Soldier, she started singing very low "I'm a no limit soldier I thought I told ya", we laughed and talked about good old school music until we saw the food headed our way. I was feeling pretty good from the Cognac, and we both were ready to chow down. I ordered lobster and salad. Mo'nae had salmon with mashed potatoes and a vegetable medley. I told Mo'nae "here we are at a Steak restaurant and neither one of us got a steak." We both laughed and plus we were having a great time talking about her, then me and the job and whatever else came to mind. We talked about what will come now that everything might get shut down due to this virus. She told me about her past relationship and I told her about mine.

First off I want to let you know that I have been divorced for two years and have a 9 year old son. I used to live with my ex-wife in Chattanooga. I came back about 3 years ago when I got offered my position at work. However I do get my son 2 weeks in July and 2 weeks during Christmas and am looking forward to it.

Mo'nae said "how sweet, maybe one day when the right man comes alone, maybe we can have two children but if he never comes then I'm fine by myself." I looked at her and said "never know when he will come do you?" She looked back at me and said "no I sure don't, the question is if he comes how will I know he's the one?" I said "that's just something we'll have to see, isn't it?" She said "We'll," I said "did I stutter?" Mo'nae gave me a look that was hard to read, and then a smirk. (Yea she liked what i said.) We finished eating and got another drink while we sat and talked.

I am really feeling Mo'nae. She seems to be down to earth and knows what she wants. I feel like she has been straight with me and I know I have been good with her. I know I'm going to ask her out again and I can't wait to see what she says when I do. Finally, we were getting ready to leave when she jumped and turned around like she saw a ghost or something. I asked her if everything was okay and for about 10 seconds she froze, then she looked around at me and said "yes I just had a head rush, I guess too much tequila".

Heading to the car, I asked if she was sure she was fine because she shook with fear the whole walk. Monae said yes "I'm fine, I just needed this fresh air I guess." I looked at my watch and it was 9:10. I then asked her if she was enjoying herself. Monae answered "sure I did, is it over?" I told her not if she didn't want it to be and asked if was she up for a ride? She said yes, so I decided to drive up to The Mint @Kentucky Downs just to check out the new little Casino they have. It was about a 45 minute drive which I was in no hurry to get to. I was just enjoying her presence and conversation.

We arrived at what has to be one of the smallest casinos in the world, she just sat there at first like she didn't want to get out. She turned and looked at me and said Thanks so much. I know we haven't done much, but you have no clue how thankful I am just to be able to be out with a real man. I said, ``A real man please explain?" Monae was just telling me about in the past how within the first hour sex would have been the topic with the other guys. Monae explained how glad she was that we didn't talk about it and we've been together now for a good 3 hours. I told her well I got way more on my mind than sex, that's never important until both people are ready for it and I really don't want to talk about it now, so if you're ready lets go in so I can see what skills you have on these machines and tables. She told me that she had never been to a casino and didn't have a clue on what to do. I told her that was great because she would have beginner's luck. To my surprise that's exactly what she had. Her first machine she hit for 350 and put her money in her pocket. We walked around for a little while because I like to play the tables and they didn't have a single table game in the place. An hour or so had passed and I asked if she was ready to go and she said yes if you are. On our way out of the casino she told me to stick out my hand and she had her hand in a ball and placed a piece of rolled up paper in my hand. As I unfolded I saw that it was 50 dollars, I said no I can't take your money. Monae said "look we came here to win and I couldn't let you walk out of this place not a winner". I told her not to take your money back, I was a winner before I got here. She looked confused and said "what do you mean?" I told her I won when you told me that you would go out with me. Monae gave me that sexy shy smile and put her arm around me all the way to the car.

On my way to take her home it took longer because I took the long way. Once back into town I drove around Downtown Nashville just to see the wild drunk people and their country music playing loud from the different bars on the strip. I turned down my music just so we could hear all the noise around the car. One couple walked in front of the car and yelled at me; Man you have one pretty lady right there, the woman hollered Hell Yeah she's hot...I looked over at Monae and said wow we must look like a couple and gave my best smile (all teeth.) Mo'nae said "I guess we do, so I guess that means we have to do this again." I was stunned because she just asked me out before I could ask her again. Talking about a brother looking like aww shit now.

I didn't want the night to end but I couldn't wait for the next day either so I headed to her place to drop her off and again she asked if

I wanted to come in for a night cap. I answered quickly, "Of course I would but I can't stay long. I've got a busy morning."

We got to her place, I walked Mo'nae in while holding her hand. First thing she did was kick off her shoes and headed to the bar. When she sat down beside me I told her I just had deja vu, she asked why. I think it's the way you smell like I've smelled it before. Mo'nae laughed saying that she put on the oil because I commented on it a long time ago. As I drank my drink I asked if I could rub her feet since that was the first thing she did and kicked off those heels when we walked in. She told me that I didn't have to but I insisted that I wanted to and it was no bother to me. We had a good conversation and I made sure that she was relaxed from my great foot massage, then I realized it was time for me to bounce. I gave Mo'nae a nice long hug and we shared how perfect our night was. I told her I would call tomorrow as I walked to the door. Monae walked with me and right before I walked out she grabbed me and hugged me tight and said Thanks Again. I told her that was the last thanks and she stood on her toes and kissed me on the cheek. Woo wasn't expecting that but I liked it. I told her I promised to call her tomorrow and I left out the door. I must admit I wanted to stay and give her this Good, Good but that wasn't part of my plan not yet.

Chapter 13

How Stella got her groove back was on and it was at the part where she and Winston were making love in the shower. What a steamy scene and it made me think about what if all these times Calvin has come into my house these last few weeks that we've been quarantined, wondering if he can make me feel like her. So there I was with my toy getting ready to go at it when the phone rang. I looked at the caller id this time by my bed and it was the same number ending in 6969 from that man with the voice. This spooked me out because it's like he calls every time I get horny. I answered the phone and put it on speaker, the sexy deep voice tells me don't talk just listen, like he was Jodeci or some damn body. He said to me; "your body called for me again, and I'm answering it. I want to make it feel what it's been longing for". I just laid there listening and lusting at the sound of his voice. Then he said "I want to lick you everywhere, starting at your wettest spot and working my way all over until you tell me to stop. Even if you said stop, your body will show the signs for me to keep going. Matter of fact I'm going to make sure you can't speak. However, I will allow you to moan with pleasure so just lay back and let my tongue do the talking." I was so quiet you could hear a pin drop in my house. My hands started rubbing my nipples and my temp was going up at this time. He said "help me fulfill this craving that I have for you, allow me to taste you. Do this one thing for me and I promise you will want me to keep coming, I mean keep you cumin." I laid there thinking damn that sounds so good, as I let the tip of the dildo rub against my clit, slowly turning it to the lowest vibration so that he can't hear it. The voice said "when you're ready leave the door unlocked for me and I promise you won't regret it. I'm coming for one thing and that is a taste but my goal will be to satisfy your pussy with the tongue and the tongue with your pussy. You get that baby?" "Yes" I said as if he was right there with me, forgetting that he could hear me. I put a pillow over the dildo and now I'm at full speed letting this dildo and this voice take me to the moon, after I came so hard twice. I caught a cramp in my damn leg because my body was so stiff with pleasure. I picked up the phone breathing heavily and said why are you doing this to me, not letting him know that I'm so turned on by him, his voice and the things he wants to do to me. He told me that he wasn't doing anything, it was me. He said, "When you're ready, unlock the door and he hangs up the phone. I dialed the number back and I got a message that the voicemail has not been set up. In a sense I was pissed that I couldn't finish my conversation with this man. I don't know what to do about this. I'm so turned on by the thought of having this strange person calling me but then again it makes me strange if I like it. Damn this can be a very dangerous game if not played right, I don't want Calvin to know about the man with the voice but I really want to take him up on his offer, man oh man what do I do? How can I get away with it? I want to be pleased, I want to be loved and I know that Calvin can possibly give me that love but I can't give Calvin my body yet because I'm scared. On the other hand the freak in me wants to be pleased by a complete stranger. Damn I'm in between a rock and a hard place. This 60 day rule that I made up may be way over my head. I need some dick now and I'm not sure if I'm going to be able to hold back any longer. Frustrated, I turned over, got in my favorite sleeping position and went to sleep.

Chapter 14

CALVIN

Since our 3rd and 4th date went perfect, I decided to call Mo'nae to see if she wanted to go to a nice little jazz club not too far from the building she works at. See I never told her that I owned "The Spot" I just don't want to seem as if I'm bragging about what all I got. I have all plans to let her know as soon as we get there. See Mo'nae is not like any woman I've dated; she is the complete opposite. She has offered to pay for my meals a couple of times when we were out this last month. Being the man that I am, how could I let her.

Mo'nae told me that she would be happy to go out, as long as we are not around a lot of people. So I went and picked her up and felt like I was the luckiest guy in the world. There she was wearing a pair of Apple Bottom jeans and I knew right then that all I wanted to do was bite that Big Round apple. The effect she had on me was unreal and one day she will know just how much. I, on the other hand, could not wait to show her.

When we arrived at the club, I pulled my car into the owner's parking place. Mo'nae asked me if I think the owner would mind me parking in his parking place. I grinned and winked at her and said I won't mind. She looked at me and said this is your club? " She says "why didn't you tell me?" With my best sexiest look I said to her, "I just did" as I reached for the door handle to get out the car. Mo'nae sat back and watched me as I came in front of the car to open the door for her. So, she said Da' Spot...mmm...I like it already and I grabbed her hand and we went in. All my people greeted her as if she were a celebrity. She was shocked at the attention she received as we made our way to my private booth. I asked Mo'nae if she wanted something to drink, and she said water for now. The waitress brought her water and I got a bud light beer. We sat and listened to the band play. Mo'nae asked me why I kept this place a secret. I told her it's no secret I just didn't think it was that important and I knew that she was for sure going to be my special guest. She asked how did everyone know her name? Come on Mo'nae you are the special lady in my life, shit thinking to myself *hope she feels the same way too.* Mo'nae response was shocking; she actually said "okay I can accept that answer." I slid next to her and kissed her on her neck and I told her that I would be right back, I went in the back and spoke to my good friend Darrin and came right back to the table to my beautiful woman. Since Corona Virus was running shit, there were only 10 other people in the club not counting the 4 band members. Darrin announced that a special request had been made and started to sing, "If this world were mine" by Luther Vandross.

I handed my Queen a rose, stuck out my hand, and asked my angel to dance. At first she hesitated, and then put her hand in mine as we walked to the dance floor. I felt like President Obama dancing with my own Flotus. Mo'nae looked me in the eye and said "it had been a long time since she danced." I told her that if I have anything to do with it I hope it will not be our last time. Mo'nae whispered in my ear that this was her favorite song, then she put her head on my chest and relaxed as we enjoyed each other's presence. Even when Darrin stopped singing we didn't leave the floor. The DJ took over and the next song came on was R Kelly's Slow Jam and then you hear "Hey Mr. DJ." I don't know one person who would just go sit down on back to back jams like these. After we finished dancing I told her to follow me and said let me show you something. We walked to the back of the club and got on the elevator. I entered my code then pushed the top floor button; that's what the button said. When the elevator doors opened, we were in my luxury suite. She asked once again this is yours too? I said yes this is where I live; believe it or not no other females have ever been here but you. Mo'nae twisted her mouth to say yea right, then she smiled and said just kidding. "No really" I said I just got this remodeled about 3 months ago and the club part has been open for 4 months. Mo'nae walked around for a while and looked at my place as if she was looking for any signs of another woman. She looked at me and said "Not bad for a single guy." I told her "yea. but no for long." Then I opened up the side door to the balcony and told Mo'nae to come out with me. We stared at each other a little and then I put my arm around her. I told her that she was beautiful and how I had wanted to take her out for at least a year. She asked why I never said anything; I told her I wanted to wait till the time was right and for some reason I felt it was time. I told her that I didn't want to rush into anything but that maybe if she was really feeling this then we could eventually take this to the next level. I hugged her and started to squeeze her and the harder I hugged the more she moaned and quickly told me it's time for her to go. I asked if she would like to take the stairs instead of the elevator since we were already outside, she said "next time I'd be glad to take the stairs up and down." I looked at her and said "oh so there will be a next time." "She said hell yes you already said I was your woman not taking that back." I closed the door and we walked back over to the elevator. Mo'nae turned to me and kissed me lightly on the lips and pushed the down button on the elevator. We got off the elevator and before we got to the door Mo'nae told me to hold on a minute and went to the bar. She ordered a beer for me and a shot of tequila for herself, she asked "what time does this place close?" I told her at 12am since I can't have more than 20 people at a time here due to state regulation and the CV. why? I asked. Mo'nae said "no reason just trying to see how many more drinks I can order." I told her as much as you want but I can't be drinking that much so I have to take you home. Mo'nae looked at me and said "who said I was going anywhere?" I said "you just said up the stairs," she cut me off... "Stop bringing up old shit" and then burst out laughing. I have to admit she made me nervous, hell she is taking shots like a pro and she seems really comfortable.

So comfortable that she was LIT, after about an hour and 4 shots later I asked Mo'nae was she ready to go home? Mo'nae said yes if home is going back up on the elevator. I knew it had to be the liquor talking, so I told Darrin he was in charge of shutting the club down cause Mo'Nae and I were calling it a night. I grabbed Mo'nae by her hand and led her back up to my apartment. Mo'nae went into a mode that I just wasn't expecting. She took everything off except her matching black bra and panties and asked me "what do you think?" At first I was speechless and then in my faint voice I told her, "I think you are the most beautiful woman in the world." I walked over to her and asked her "are you sure about this? " She answered with a deep breath and said "more than you will ever know." I picked her up and walked into my bedroom, she grabbed my head and started kissing me so passionately. I was so turned on by this beauty, I laid her on my bed and kissed her from her neck to her breast. Mo'nae moaned and asked if she could feel me inside her. I told her not to rush, I've got all the time in the world because I didn't want to miss a spot on her body. Mo'nae was saying how good I was making her feel, how my lips were causing her nipples and clit to ache in ecstasy. I couldn't help it, Her pheromone was causing my Jaws to tingle, I had to taste her. I slipped her panties off and the smell of her pussy was captivating. I went head first into her, kissing all around and sucking any juice that may have seeped out from her pink flower. I turned my head sideways so that my lips would line up with her lips and kissed her pussy as if I was sucking her lips on her face. Mo'nae screamed out as she came quickly. She grabbed the back of my head and pulled my face in as deep as she could. Then I felt this gush all over my face, my queen had just squirted all in and on my face and mouth. Damn baby I said I raised up to thank her for her fruit juice. I told her that her smell was intoxicating and it caused me to feel a buzz. Mo'nae mumbled "this is just like the phone conversation" and then she never said another word. She laid there shaking and after a moan and a Oh My God she fell straight to sleep. I was cool with that. I knew the liquor was talking and I gave her what she wanted from him. I cleaned her up and put her on a pair of my boxers and covered her up. Yes, those panties belong to me now. I laid down beside her with her personal perfume all over my face and watched her sleep until I fell out.

Chapter 15

I woke up at 10:00 am, Calvin was sitting there looking at me. I felt embarrassed because I really don't remember what happened and why I'm in his bed. I asked "why do I have on your boxers OMG what did I do?" Calvin said I gave him my panties and I took his boxer just so we could have something of each other. Calvin just smiled and said "No we didn't have sex." I asked, "What did we have?" He said "well I had dessert and you my dear had a good night's sleep." I felt like I could have crawled under something, "you mean we started but I went to sleep?" Calvin said "yes but that's fine the shots of tequila kind of had a hold on you but you have nothing to be ashamed of. You were still a Lady, just a very sexy and wet one." I told Calvin that I was sorry for falling to sleep on him and that I will make it up one day. He said "one day, okay I'll be waiting." I grabbed my clothes and kissed Calvin and told him I had to leave, today was Best friend day. Meaning that I needed Tina so I could vent. He said "that's fine baby, let's go." I told him "No and that I would Uber home." Calvin asked me if I was sure and I told him yes. I will be fine, we hugged and kissed for eternity then told him that I'll see you later. While walking down the stairs, I felt my coochie tingle in a good way and some memories started to play back in my mind. I remember his lips making me come hard. OMG that's all I could think I can't believe what I've done, but it was so damn good well what I remember.

I got out of the Uber in front of my house, I called my friend Tena, she was still sleeping but who gives a damn, not I. "Get your ass up," I told Tena. She said "fuck you." I told her "you wish." Tena said "no Freak you're not my type." I asked "what do you have planned for today?" Tena said "not shit really, what's up?" I said "get up, wash your ass, brush your breath and I'll be there in an hour to get you." Tena said "who said I was going somewhere?" I told her "me and I got something to tell you that I'm sure you want to hear." Tena said "like what?" I said "about a man that I have been going out with for a month." Tena said "what! I'm getting up right now and you better be here in 58 minutes, bye heifer." I hung up the phone and took my shower. I put on a T-shirt with leggings and my new Jordan's I got last week at sport seasons. Being out all night got me a little sore in the legs. So today I will be as comfortable as I can.

I left the house a few minutes early to get gas because it takes 30 minutes to get to Tena's house. Carlos's controlling ass moved her to Brentwood which I call the country, I guess to keep the police off his no good ass. I pulled up at the gas station and went inside to get water and to pay for my gas. I was opening the cooler door and a man walks by with a hood on his head and says in a deep voice, 'don't forget to leave the door unlocked.' I turned around startled at first and said sir what did you say, but when I said that he ran out the store. I tried to see which way he ran but he was too fast. I ran out of the store with the water in my hand and he was gone, I don't have an idea which way he went or how he got away. I wanted to see him, I needed to see the mystery man that is offering his services to my wants and needs. I stood there just looking around, then the cashier from the store came out and asked if I was going to pay for the water. I said "sorry" and turned and walked back to the store. I paid for the water and told the cashier to give me 40.00 dollars' worth of gas on pump 3, so I went out to start pumping my gas. I was still looking around to see if I could spot the black hood he was wearing. I never saw him again repeating what he said, to leave the door unlocked. I laughed at the fact that I really do want to leave it unlocked for some of that good... good. I got in the car, pulled down my visor and just looked at myself in the small mirror. I had to get myself together, I wiped off the sweat and guzzled half the water. I put on my seatbelt, started the car headed to Tena's house.

Now Tena is a complete fool. I met her ass in first grade and we have been friends since then. Tena is cool but she can be a bad refrigerator sometimes and that's why I don't tell her all my business. I love her though because no matter what she will and has always been there for me. Tena's relationship I am no fan of, but because he is this big time drug dealer and makes lots of money: she is scared that she will miss out on the next Gucci shoes, purse or whatever. Carlos doesn't beat her at least I hope he doesn't, but he talks to her pretty bad and I believe just by some of Tena and my conversations he's been cheating on her. Tena will never tell me that part but she beats around the bush about it. I keep telling her that money can't buy love and she just gets smart with me and says shit like being lonely isn't cool either. Damn I'm sounding like a bad refrigerator now...lol.

I pulled up at Tena's house at 11:15 and blew the horn. She came running out, jumped in the car and said "you are late." I said "so you will be alright." I said "hold up...Do you have that CV-19?" She said hell naw mofo, Do you? Now stop playin tell me all about this dude. Did you fuck him? Is his dick big? Did you suck his;" I stopped her ass right there. I told her "listen crazy ass girl no I didn't fuck, suck, or even kiss him." Which I can't tell her about last night. It's too early and besides she doesn't need to know everything I do. I said "Can I have a chance to tell my story?" She said "yea I guess but I'm hungry so let's stop and grab a bite." I pulled up at Sonic and that's where we sat and ate. I ordered an Extra long Chilli Cheese Coney combo with a Strawberry slush, and she ordered the Honey BBQ wings with a large water. While eating, I started to tell her about Calvin saying his name slowly and sexy while popping my mouth just being real ghetto with it. I told her how he asked me to go out with him all the way to the club scene last night but that's it. Damn come to think of it he hasn't even text me, thinking to myself hope my wild ways didn't stop him from wanting me. Tena said oh girl you sound like you got a good one, I said I think so in my excited voice. I had to describe how he looks from front to back damn near in and out because she has to know it all. After she asked everything she could about him, she told me that she was happy for me and she couldn't wait to meet him. We finished eating and I told her I needed something sexy to wear because I was going to cook Calvin a candle light dinner one night soon and I want to be sexy when he comes over. Tena said "girl I got you," That's her favorite saying. She did because if she didn't know anything about anything she knew her clothes. Tena made a call to one of her connections. 10 minutes later we pulled up to a store that had everything that was meant to be sexy in it from clothes to shoes, perfumes, candles, rose petals trust me the list goes on and on. I was at one rack and Tena was at another, I looked and looked for something but everything stopped at a size 16. I need a 20 for these hips and ass, about that time Tena said "come here Mo'nae right now, I got you girl." I got over there and Tena had a beautiful Black Designer dress by Jovani that had a very low front, stopped right at the thigh and tighter than a wet bathing suit. I asked "what size is it?" She looked in and said it was a size 16-18. I said "I can't wear that." Tena said "yes you can". Grabbed me by my arm and we went over to the dressing room. Tena pretty much pushed me in the dressing room and threw the dress at me and slammed the door. I told her that I am going to get her. I took off my shirt and slipped the dress over my head. I could still see my bra so I took it off to see how the dress would look without it. "So far it's okay," I said out loud. Tena said "let me see." I stepped out and asked "you think this is too sexy?" Tena said "damn you so fucking country, why do you still have leggings on? Hell you can't see how it really looks until you take them off." So I stepped back into the room and took them off. When I looked in the mirror I couldn't believe my eyes, I looked marvelous, and it fit damn well. I came out and Tena started singing "you a five star chick" in her Trina voice. I told her to stop singing and tell me if this was the one or put it back. She said "hell to the no and if I were a man," I told her "you're not a man, so don't say shit." We laughed and Tena said "on a serious tip girl you look good, now who got you?" I told her you are my girl. We hugged and I told her "don't put makeup on my dress." I went in to take off the dress and my phone rang. I put my clothes back on fast, grabbed the phone and I had just missed a call from Calvin. Then his name jumped back in again. I answered really quickly this time.

"Hello Calvin." He says "Hey baby, What are you doing?" I answered "Nothing much, remember my girlfriend and I are out shopping a little." Calvin asked me"Are you buying me something?" I said "What do you want?" in a seductive voice. In his sexy voice he states, "You, all wrapped up in nothing at all." Mmm is all I could say. He said, "Are you okay?" I said "yes you make me weak talking like this." He said "ooh didn't mean to do that, since I'm not there to fix it with something strong." Then Calvin asked if I could go to Jared and pick up a package for him. "It should be ready under my name. Just pull up in front of the door because they are not letting anyone in. They will come out and get information and give them the passcode "Love is God." If you have any problems call me and I'll come by tonight if that's okay with you to get it." I told him that's fine with me and that I would be home about 5 this evening. Then I asked him "what are you gonna do for me?" and then said, "Just kidding." He said you will see when I get there, I told him I was just kidding and then he said well I'm not, see you soon. I said bye. Tena said "Mo'nae bring your ass out of that room, what were you doing in there?" I told her I was talking to Calvin why? Tena said "oh I thought you were stealing or playing with your stuff and shit." I said "Tina you know I don't steal don't be saying no shit like that, hell you be done got these people all upset and be done call the police on us." Headed to the register I yelled at Tena, "now you bring your ass on." Tena "said don't holler at me no damn more you ain't my momma or daddy." I told her shut the hell up and come on. The woman at the counter was shaking. I told her honey we are just playing so you don't have to be nervous, and wearing these masks didn't make it better for her. I talk to that crazy girl like that all the time. The nervous old lady rang up my dress and it came to $227.00, I said "I can't believe I'm paying this much for something that I'm just going to wear in the house for dinner." Tena said "oh shut up, that's not expensive and it's not like you got shit to do with money anyways, hell but pay the bills. We all do that, if you call yourself complaining about the price of the dress you should see how much this one cost," while holding up another dress. I told her "I'm not complaining, I just never had a reason to buy me anything this nice. Tena answered with quickness, "Calvin seems to be a Great reason so it seems." We left the store then headed over to Jared's, picking up the beautifully wrapped box for Calvin. Tena was over there asking enough questions for a court trial. I answered all of them and told her I was going to take her home and go home and chill. Tena immediately said "oh so now you are tired of me?" I said "no, I just got to go home sooner than expected." I looked at her and got really excited and said "because Calvin is coming over that's why I'm taking you home sooner." Tena said" man you must really like this guy, because you have never neglected me like this," while pouting. I told her you know I love you but I got to get to this man. We rode listening and singing to 92Q bumping ole school. Finally we pulled up at Tena's house and before she got out she said "I know you better call me later." Tena got out and I told her I would call her tomorrow and let her know how my night went. She told me she loved me and turned to go into the house. Before I knew it Carlos had run outside talking shit to Tena about not asking him if she could go anywhere. He looked at me and said to Tena "you better be glad you were with Mo'nae" or and he jumped at her. He threw his hand up at me, smiled and said "how are you doing Mo'nae?" I said "fine Carlos." I didn't even bother asking him how he was, I just pulled off.

Chapter 16

I was on my way to the house when Calvin called and "said I'm at your place getting ready to hit your buzzer". I said "I'm on the way, I just dropped my friend off and I'll be there in about 15 minutes." He said "ok that's cool have you eaten yet?" I said "earlier when I first got out but that was a few hours ago, I can go for a bite or two. You want me to pick something up while on my way home?" Calvin said "why don't you just make it here and I'll go, that will help my time pass away just sitting here waiting." In a sense he sounded like he was trying to be smart, and I think I like it. I said "that is fine, surprise me I don't discriminate against food. See you in a minute," then I hung up. I was so excited that Calvin was waiting for me until I think I sped up a little but was still driving safely. I told him I'd be home by 5 and it's 5:30 so like I said he is an on time man. I pulled up at my place and went in the house just to make sure everything was legit before he got back, and it was because that's how I keep it. I ran in my room and hung up my dress because that was his surprise for Sunday night. With the governor shutting down the city, I can't wait to be quarantined with Calvin. However, I plan to make that night a good one. I'm trying to be a good girl but it's so hard being with him and his fine ass. In my mind, I'm not ready yet but my pussy floor muscles are screaming Orgasm please; way before I even thought of a Calvin.

Okay, let me calm my hot ass down now, I took a deep breath and sat down on the couch. Just a few minutes later Calvin knocked on the door. I jumped up with much excitement and opened the door and there he stood looking like a piece of candy waiting to be unwrapped and eaten. I said "come in" while glancing at his everything. I grabbed the extra bag that looked as if he were going to drop. He took the food over to the table and said "hope you like Chinese". I said "of course I do, wasn't I supposed to buy food?" Calvin said "yep and you can give me my money back right now," while laughing. I looked at the receipt stapled on the bag and told him I got him...now I'm sounding like Tena. He said he was just playing and told me to come to him. I got up from the table and went around to him, he stood up and said "you say you got me then how are you going to forget my hug?" I hugged him and loved it just being in his arms, oh man what a feeling. I looked up at him and this time when he looked back at me he kissed me gently on the lips. He got ready to move his lips back. I licked them and stuck my tongue in his mouth. Without hesitation he tongued me right back and there we were lost in each other, until my stomach growled loud. Calvin said "damn...wasn't expecting that." I said "whew...me neither, you were getting ready to start something." Calvin said "that something has already been started just wasn't finished," then looked at me with a smirk. I said "okay I hear ya, loud and clear." Calvin told me to turn around and I asked "why?" He said "just spin around for me." I said "okay not knowing what this means." He said "those leggings were made for you." I said you think so? Calvin said "I don't know about you being my woman looking like that, I'd have to fight everyday." I said "no you will not, I'm a one man woman." He smiled and said "okay I hope so, now let's eat." That is exactly what we did. We had everything that was on the buffet. I really love the egg rolls and beef lo Mein. I tried the shrimp fried rice but didn't care much for it. The general Tso chicken was okay but not a favorite of mine, but the steak and vegetables was the bomb. Calvin ate everything, he said he loved it all. We finally finished and there was still enough to eat for tomorrow. After we finished eating I started cleaning up the kitchen and Calvin started to help. I watched his every move as he gathered all the trash and tied it up.

I reached into my purse and handed Calvin the box for Jared's. Calvin thanked me and proceeded to sit the box on the table over by the door, so he wouldn't forget it whenever he leaves. I handed Calvin 40 dollars, I said "for the food." He said "oh no, you can't pay me for this. You owe me one out on the town." I said oh well my fault, but I can do that too honey with a little ghetto neck snap. He said I'm sure you can and don't forget it because you said it. In a smart playing way, I said to Calvin "as fine as you are I would be honored to buy you dinner. Matter of fact I want you to come over Sunday and watch the new Quiet Place II movie with me, I'll fix dinner and plus I have a surprise for you later afterwards." Calvin said "really well what a coincidence; I have a surprise for you too." I looked at him, as to say whatever. I said "you can't have a surprise for me because I got one for you". Calvin said "well I had my surprise first but you told me about yours before I had the chance to tell you about mine." I said "ok we will see Sunday want we?" he said "sure will." We sat down on the couch and I asked Calvin "what he had up for tonight?" he said "nothing, why?" I told him I had the three Twilight movies and I never saw them and asked if he wanted to watch one with me. Calvin said "cool, turn it on." I dimmed the lights and turned on the movie hoping that it was scary, I moved closer to him and he motioned for me to get even closer. So there we were cuddled all up with each other watching the movie.

The 2nd movie had gone off when Calvin awoke me. I looked at the clock and it was 1:00 o'clock a.m. I slipped from under Calvin's arm and as soon as I stood up he said "where do you think you are going?" I said "to the restroom, do you realize what time it is, right?" Calvin looked at his watch and said "damn time flies when you're having fun." Heading to the bathroom, I said "how would you have fun if I was sleeping?" Calvin said "because I was able to hold you, that's the part that made it fun for me. Oh by the way, the movie was really good. I can't wait to see the next part." I came out of the bathroom and said "Calvin you are the reason I went to sleep. Being in your arms made me feel so comfortable and your warm body made me relax. So that was all your fault." Calvin stood up and walked over to me and said "this is all your fault" and grabbed me by the back of my head and tried sticking his whole face down my throat. Kissing me so passionately until all I could think was that we are about to fuck right here, yes it's about to go down. I moved back to get a good deep breath while saying to him, "I'm so turned on, I don't want you to leave please stay with me tonight." Calvin said "no I can't tonight, trust me baby I'm the one not ready yet. I'm sorry I kissed you like that. I was wrong and in no way trying to take advantage of you." I said "you don't have to apologize for anything. I wanted you to kiss me and so much more. I don't want you to feel pressured about anything either. Calvin, the feelings I have for you are true and I want us to be on the same level in everything we do." Calvin said "Thank you Mo'nae I really care about you as well and I want that time to be very special for both of us, now give me a hug so I can get out of here." I leaned into his chest so hard I could feel his heartbeat. I told Calvin that I couldn't wait to see him again and have a good night. We only gave each a peck on the lips as he said goodnight and walked out the door. Guess you know what I did......

Chapter 17

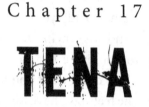

"Tena…Tena get your ass up, Carlos said in his early morning angry voice. Why come you sleep so late you know I got shit to do. You're such a lazy bitch at times, I'm about to start hating your fucking ass." "I said Carlos, I don't feel like getting up. I'm tired because you kept me up too long last night." "Carlos' response was, "Bitch you know my dad is coming here today and I need you to entertain him while I run this shit to Oklahoma." "I told Carlos, damn you don't have to talk to me like that, remember you're the one who needs me to do something for you." Carlos grabbed me by my lower jaw then said "I'm going to teach you a lesson" and started punching me as if he were giving me a whooping and talking at the same time. Saying shit like "bitch when I tell you to do something you don't wait until you're ready you do it, you do it right then, Do I Make Myself Clear?" Crying, "Yes Carlos, I'm sorry please stop." By the time he was done with me. I had a black eye and my arm was hurting like no other pain I have ever felt. As Carlos was leaving his dad pulled in the driveway. I didn't clean myself up or anything. I wanted his dad to see what he had just done to me. Mr. Daniels came in and said "oh child, what did he do to you?" As he reached for my arm I let out a loud scream. Mr. Daniels told me that he knew of a doctor that would come to the house and look at my arm because he wouldn't feel right taking me to the hospital knowing that they would call the police to have his son locked up. I looked at him thinking you old bastard you thinking about your son going to jail and I'm the one sitting here fucked up by the hands of your son. We sat in silence for about 30 minutes until Dr. Trevor came right over and tended to my wounds. He confirmed that my arm was broken, put it in a splint and said that he would come back in two days to put a cast on it then told me that the black eye would go away in a couple of weeks. He gave me a lortab 10 and wrote a prescription for 30 more. I thanked the Dr. for coming and I took the pill. Mr. Daniels got a warm rag. He began to wipe my face and in the mist he began rubbing my thigh saying how N.J and Chris told him how good my pussy was and he would hate to tell Carlos about it. After all that, I knew where this was going, this fucking old ass dime dropper. I hate a mutherfucking snitch. So I laid there crying feeling the effects of the Lortab 10 and letting this old man fuck me with his wrinkled dick going in and out of my dry pussy, "Fuck Viagra". When he finished he sucked his entire nut out of me and nutted on himself as he did it. He said he hadn't tasted himself in a while and didn't want to leave any evidence. That made me sick to my stomach and ran into the bathroom, threw up and let the hot water from the shower run all over my body until the water turned cold. I feel like I'm damned, everything happens to me and like a fool I just take this shit. I scrubbed my body like I was trying to take my skin off. I hate what I have become; I'm nobody but the dope man's bitch and his family's mattress. It is time for a change. I can't keep doing this. While in deep thought and lots of tears I heard, "Tena are you ok?" Mr. Wrinkle dick asked. I wouldn't say anything, I just continued to scrub my body. Eventually after about an hour or so I came out and the bastard was gone.

Chapter 18

I was awakened by the soft juicy kisses to my feet, I wanted to tell Calvin to stop but I couldn't. I thought damn he's good, how he got my pajamas off I'll never know. I lay there with my eyes closed enjoying every lick, suck, and kiss, all I could do was moan uncontrollably. Thinking damn this better not be a wet dream. I knew better once he moved up to my thighs, oh shit my pussy began to jump with a beat of its own. After kissing both the inner and outer parts of my thighs, Calvin moved to my pussy. I almost lost it. He kissed it slowly all over, and then with the width of his tongue he began licking it like it was no tomorrow. I couldn't hold it any more. I started coming; he knew it too because he then began to drink the flow of my river. He was moaning like it was better than chicken and was licking me clean. He grabbed my clit and licked around it slowly, my body quivered. I screamed in exhilarating joy letting him know that I was coming again. He never let go of my clit; he just kept right on eating my pussy for what seemed like forever. I grabbed the back of his head so hard to pull him in closer to me until I could feel his jaws moving from the back of his head. I came again the more I pulled him into my wet pussy the more he wanted; every time I came he would slurp me. I told Calvin to let me cum all over his dick. I was begging for the dick. In a whisper he told me to keep my eyes closed. I had no problem with that because this feeling that I have has me incoherent. He entered my pussy sideways. All I could do was call out to the Good Lord above. The curve in his dick had me wanting to spin around on it. I was in awe, It felt so good. All Calvin did was whispered you are everything I knew you would be. This is mine, say it. Tell me this is mine. As he stroked deeper into my uterus, his arms around me tightly. I could tell he wanted to cum with me. I promise I squeezed his dick with this pussy as hard as I could knowing that when I spoke the words (It is yours) that I was going to cum so hard. I could not resist. I was so ready to cum, I told him, "It's All Yours" while releasing my juices all over his dick. He pulled me into him. I felt like our souls touched as he went into Beast Mode knowing I was cumming he didn't hold back. He nutted real good and hard in my pussy. We both were throbbing so hard. I told him in between my deep breaths that that was the best I ever had. Eyes still closed because of the intense Stimulation I began to kiss him. The kiss was a little different than before. I softly spoke his name to tell him how I've never felt this good. As I began to open my eyes I was confused because this person was not Calvin. He looked darker and bigger and the darkness of my room was not helping me see any better. His deep voice said "I help you release the Oxytocin from your brain and you call me him."

I yelled while pushing him up, then jumped up and ran across the room. I couldn't scream or anything from the shock. I asked "who the fuck are you?" His deep voice said "you left the door open for me, I gave you exactly what you wanted and you gave me what I needed." Speechless, I didn't know how to feel since I had just experienced the best sex that I could remember ever. I couldn't see his face as hard as I tried. I guess it was because he grabbed his dark clothes and covered his face as He walked closer to the door and said "next time you wanna cum, Cum to me, I'll make that happen."

The mystery man opened the door and left. I ran quickly and locked the door, still shaking, soaking wet by what just happened. I slid down the wall to the floor and asked myself if this is really what I want. I thought about Calvin and said OMG what have I done. Then it hit me. Last night when he left I was so horny until all I was thinking about was making me cum and I forgot to lock my damn door. How stupid can one be? So does that mean that he was checking my door every night? I jumped up and grabbed my cell phone getting ready to call Calvin Then I thought what the fuck am I going to say to him and it's only 4:30 in the morning. I remember when he told me to leave the door unlocked, but hell I wasn't going to really do it. I did this shit to myself, now I'm scared and Pleased at the same fucking time. I don't know how to feel, I don't know what to say or who to tell, Fuck now I'm paranoid. I'm not on birth control and he came all in me so deep. What have I done again I say as I burst out in tears, not knowing that this could completely change my life forever.

Chapter 19

This woman is incredible, the love I have for her is not heard of well maybe it is just not seen as much these days. That feeling she gave me is like no other. I had to leave because she made me nervous. She makes my stomach shake, my knees weak and my heart races. I have never held anything back from anyone until now. I want Monae to know that I want all of her, not just a little bit. For the first time in my life I know that I'm in love, I finally understand the difference between obsession and love. I felt the love when I fucked her real good and made her feel all of me. Her insides were as hot as flames, burning for my love. I wanted her to feel like no other. Her Juices quenched my dry spots and her pussy fit me perfectly. Just knowing the our air from fucking her is sweet, that confirms we are meant to be.

I don't know what to do about my secret and the fact that she doesn't know that I know about hers. It has me excited in ways that even I don't understand. I don't want to hide anything from her if we are going to have a relationship. The fantasies that I long for are just about where they need to be, to be fulfilled. Once my fantasy has been fulfilled then I can go ahead with the life that we will plan together. At least I hope we can plan a life together. The fact of being the man of mystery and being Calvin the cool loving guy turns me on just as much as watching her pleasure herself thinking about me or the other me. I know she is in need of love but the lust that she wants from the man with the voice is something so sexual that even I don't believe I can fulfill, as Calvin. In a way I do want her to tell me about him; which is me, but on the other hand I want her to tell me about her fantasy and how she wants me to be the one to fulfill it. I really enjoyed the way she tasted, felt, smell, her moaning sounds, just all of the above. I, as him, want her to enjoy the necessities of every pleasure point on her body given by him. Me as Calvin wants her to let me be the one who meets all her wishes and needs. This may sound crazy but in a way I think I'm jealous of him. What am I to do? How do I give her the best of both worlds? I have to come up with a plan so that she will know that I'm the only one for her. I guess when you live a double life you have to deal with the double consequences of trying to be more than you really are. I can't hold back any longer. I have to saturate my manhood as Calvin with her nectar sooner than later. The way she asked for me when I was full-filling my taste buds with her juices. I know she needs it badly. When I give it to her as myself and not him, I will not stop. I will pleasure her until she falls out. I'm trying to be better than him. That's my goal. I'm going for a T.K.O. Teddy Pendergrass ain't got nothing on me. I know what I want and now I know what to do to get it.

Finally I will get my prize. The plan will have to be better than The voice because she let it be known that the pussy was his. What if she doesn't say it's mine, What if i'm not as good as the voice? I would feel some type of way about that, because I know as him what she needs but as Calvin I'm trying to be all too damn good and want her to take as much time as she wants. Fuck this, Her little special night is when I'm going to go all out I'm going to fuck her brains out I will do everything thing I've done as the voice and see how she reacts then. If she doesn't say anything or come clean about him. Guess what I won't either.

Chapter 20

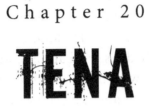

Now that the city is really shutting down little by little, I wanted to go out because it had been a month or so since the Coronavirus had hit our country hard. Carlos said that we were going on a date. Not knowing that He had bought me a Short Yellow skirt with a matching black and yellow Nappa Leather Jacket made by Prada. I had on a pair of Patent Leather Pumps and a matching handbag. To make a long story short I was Prada down. Carlos likes for me to dress very classy when I'm out with him. He was looking damn good with his Gucci Mini GG Jacket with velvet details and matching pants. While rocking the fresh ass pair of Gucci Ace GG high top sneakers. Yes we are Rated PG, but I'm ready to be Rated X cause Carlos's swag is turning me the fuck on.

I knew this was going to be exciting because he pulled out the All Black 2020 Range Rover. We cruised around for a minute until we got down town to the Renaissance Hotel. He pulled in and the valet came and opened my door. Carlos met me on my side of the car and grabbed my hand. I was so shocked because this is no way Carlos style at all. All I could think is *this nigga done fucked up now he trying to impress me with all this luxery shit, well it's working.* We went over to the elevators and stepped in. Carlos told me he had a surprise for me and told me to trust him as he pulled out a blindfold. Thinking again *surely he didn't have me to dress up to kick my ass or throw me from a window* because I noticed the ride up was a long one. I could hear the beeps of each floor we passed on the way up. Finally the elevator stopped and the programmed voice spoke saying "29th floor."

Carlos took me by my hand and led me until we stopped at what I assumed was our room. When he grabbed me by my shoulders and said "take 5 steps forward." I could hear music softly playing in the background but was still a little nervous because this is so different from the Carlos I was used to. He took off the blindfold and had me open my eyes. He had reserved an Executive Suite and our own personal chef. Candles were lit all over the suite. As we walked in, the Chef asked if there was anything else we needed. Carlos told him Thank you and that we were good. The chef told us to have a good evening and walked out the room. Carlos walked over to the table and pulled my chair out for me to sit down. He then walked over and sat in his chair. On the table was Salad, Fruit, Baked Potatoes, wine and Wagyu Beef. I looked at him and said "all this for me?" Carlos said, "Yes baby and it's long overdue." I said thank you baby and got up to kiss him. He told me to just stay there and eat and could thank him later. When I tell y'all this steak is the best steak in the world. Hell everything on this table was the bomb. I'm trying my best to act like a lady cause he is truly showing out tonight. After we finished eating I was getting ready to try some fruit, Carlos got up from the table, took the Big Ass strawberry from my hand and said "let me try it first." Carlos took me over to the King size bed and sat me down on it. I was looking at him sideways because he went and got a chair and sat in front of me, I asked "What is going on?" Carlos had me lay back on the bed as he pulled down my thong and rubbed the strawberry all over my pussy. I moaned and said "damn baby." Carlos bit the berry and put it to my mouth so I could taste. "Damn that tastes good and sweet" I said, as he pushed my skirt up and went to eat this strawberry flavored pussy. After I came real slow in his mouth he licked it all up, slapped me on the ass and said "okay let's go." I said "What, where?" He said "the night is just beginning, we will come back here later." Dazed and confused, I just went alone with whatever he was doing. I don't want to mess up tonight and make him mad.

We got back down to the lobby and while waiting for the valet, he told the bartender at the bar to hook me up with a quick shot of something good. I don't know what he gave me but it hit me real quick. Carlos was laughing at me saying "you are getting old, you can't hang like you used to." I must say he might be right."

I must say this is one of the best times I've ever had with Carlos. He actually treated me like a queen. It all seems very strange for him because just a little over a week ago he kicked my ass but I guess I've been a good girl and haven't given him a reason to bruise my face and make my account balance go up. Anyways, we left and went over to his mom's house, as we pulled up in the driveway; and I do mean drive way because Carlos and his brother had brought their mom and dad a mansion, it sat about a mile away from the main street. I mean if I had their kind of money, then I would do the same for my parents. Marble was all over the house. Furniture was flown in from Paris. Gold trimmed the staircase all the way to the third floor. Let's just say eight bedrooms and 10 bathrooms. There was a party room on the first floor in the back of the house, you could sat another house in that room alone. I noticed while we drove up to the house that there were a lot of cars over here, so just from the look of it there was a party going on; and I like to party. We got in the house and everybody was having a ball. Dancing, laughing, eating and swimming whatever; you name it. Carlos told me to get comfortable and have a good time. I went and spoke to his mother Ms. Emma and she introduced me to her friends and then I took a deep breath and spoke to Mr. Daniels. He just had to ask me for a hug. I did it because of the look on his face that said I'm going to tell, if you don't. I played it all off and got the hell away from that old pervert. I was headed toward the kitchen to get a drink and that's when I noticed N.J. and Chris sitting by the door. I quickly turned to get away before they saw me and ran smack dead into Rico. "I'm sorry" I said, he said "no need to be," while bending over to pick up the broken bottle of Budweiser I knocked out his hand. I felt my stomach go into knots seeing all these guys here and knowing that I fucked them all. Rico told me to don't worry about the mess and that he would have the maid to clean it up. I told Rico to let Carlos know that I would be right back and rushed to the bathroom to try and get myself together. This is too much for me and I need to make up an excuse to get out of here. I was actually so scared I peed a little in my panties and I thought about going out the bathroom window. The bathroom was equipped with everything you could possibly think of, almost as if in a hotel. Towels, robes, wash cloths, and every type of soap ever sold. I took a washcloth and cleaned myself up real good and changed my panties (I keep a new pair in my purse at all times). I made sure my hair was good and touched up my makeup due to all the sweat from being overwhelmed with all the Fucked and Sucked dicks in the house by me. For the first time in my life I feel like a whore but sometimes love, lust and money can make a Bitch do some crazy things. While looking in the mirror I repeated over and over "I will do better, I will be better, I am better. Yes, I am a better woman today-forever!"

I came out of the bathroom to a quiet party with everybody looking at me and Carlos was standing with his dad on one side and N.J, Chris and Rico was on the other. My heart almost fell on the ground. I looked around at everybody's expressions and I could not read them. I looked at Carlos and asked "what's going on?" He said "baby this party is for us" and got down on his knees. Carlos began to speak so softly to me looking deep into my eyes saying "Tena you are everything that I need to complete my life. My dreams came true when I met you and I love you more than life itself. It's because you've made me the man that I am today. Tena everything that I've ever done or said to you that has hurt you in any way I am sorry, I know you are a good woman and I hope that you can forgive me for all the wrong I've done and the pain I've caused. From this day forward I promise to be the best man ever only to you and only for you. So do me this favor and make me the happiest man on Earth. Marry me Tena and I promise you will not regret it." I had no idea that this is what Carlos had planned all night. I looked around and the only eyes that seemed to connect with mine were all the men I've fucked with and each one of them looked as if they were happy for me and Carlos. I smiled so hard that my jaws started to hurt. I turned to Carlos and said "yes baby yes I will marry you." Everybody clapped and yelled and the party was back on. All the females were crowded around me looking at the 5 carat chocolate diamond ring that Carlos put on my finger. I looked around to see where he was and he was sitting there with his boys smiling, talking and looking straight at me. After about 30 minutes of Carlos' and I watching each other like two teenagers in love, he walked my way, he got to me and said come on let's go and finish our own party. We said our goodbyes and headed to our destiny on the 29th floor.

Chapter 21

TENA

After our Wonderful engagement party and Awesome night at the hotel. We came back to the house a little early because once again Carlos has a drop to make. After kissing me so passionately he left out with a big smile on his face. I'm still in awe and I just can't explain this feeling that I have about this whole engagement thing. I mean I am happy but then again I'm not sure that it's real. Then again at times Carlos is a good guy when he wants to be and I think he does want to learn how to love me but just everything we have been through is not old at all. Some things still feel like it was just yesterday's ass whooping, like this cast on my arm. I'm still questioning if his love is genuine, but hell when we got back to the hotel the last night we made love for hours, he treated me as his Queen. Which he was right he should have been doing that way before now.

What really fucked me up is when I went to the refrigerator to get me something to drink. I opened up the refrigerator door and there on the top shelf was a bright red box with a bow on it and my name attached. The note on the box read; Just in case you have any doubt. I forgot about the drink because I had to see what was in this box. With much anticipation, I pulled out the box and sat it on the table and opened it. Inside was a big yellow envelope, on the front he had written Sealed with a Kiss. I'm thinking shit, *what the kiss of death*. To my surprise I opened it and it was 5 debit cards and checkbooks, and balances to all his well kept secret accounts, OMG I have access to all of his bank accounts. I started sweating, my heart started beating real hard and my brain was running 1000 miles an hour. See I knew he had money but now I see that he has Loooong Money. 5 different accounts and the account with the least is $500,000. Can you say JACKPOT!!!!

Since we have been together Carlos has never let me in, when I say in I mean in like this. I never knew how much money he had, he never even took me to the bank with him so that I wouldn't even know which banks had his money. Really my intentions was only to fuck for a few bucks, but I started catching feeling and shit. So here I am now engaged and I really need a reality check, all my life I never had to struggle for anything and trust me for some people the struggle is real. I know I don't have kids and I should have a job to get my own but that's not the way my life happened.

See all because I was this pretty young thing with a big ass, men would volunteer to give me money. No, I never had to do anything so I got accustomed to it. Like one day when I was 13, I was in the pool hall to turn in the numbers for my mom. This Big Time drug dealer was there and he said to me "hey you" I turned and looked at him and he said "yea you." I frowned at him and said "what?" He said "just cause you look so damn good I'm going to leave this here for you", and laid a 100 dollar bill on the pool table then he walked out the door. Everyone was looking at me like shit you don't want it. I looked around at everybody and said oh well and I walked my happy ass right over there and picked that bill up with the quickness. Then everyday I would go just to see if I would run into him, and I did. Eventually we started seeing each other secretly, but he would not touch me until I was old enough because he was 14 years my senior. He gave me everything I could ever imagine for years until one day he was robbed and killed. So I never really knew what a job was or even how to survive on my own because I never had to do anything but be cute. So when I met Carlos I saw the same thing in him, My source of income.

My goal was to take his money and run, but after 5 years of taking ass beating for money. I now have access to it all, Pinch me because all of this is too good to be true. My head is still not wrapping around this y'all. My heart is heavy because of my true intentions and now it was all handed to me. Part of me wants to take the money and dip but the other part of me is feeling like love may be in the air. This is a hard one even though I know I should be happy but you know the saying that money can't buy me love but in this case it just might do the job for me? Okay, sounds like it is time for a true talk with my best-friend. I know she will tell me how to handle all of this. Everything is happening so fast I just don't know what to do.

Chapter 22

CALVIN

Oh man where did I put that box, I know I didn't forget it over at Mo'nae house. It's got to be over here somewhere. Now my phone is ringing, I looked at it and it's mom, I will call her back. I have to find that box. Again the phone rang and again it was my mom. I answered it and told her I needed to call her back and that I was pretty busy looking for something. Mother says "is it in a pretty Gold Box?" I said "yes mom how do you know?" Mom said "because when you bought my groceries earlier I found this box in here, I opened it and it sure is a beautiful necklace in it. Is it mine?" Mother said with much excitement. I felt bad knowing that I was about to disappoint my mom, and I guess I took too long to answer and mom said "Boy are you still here?" I said "yes ma'am, sorry mom." She said "don't be, now this doesn't look like anything you would give your mother and then she said she must be very special." I said to mom "she really is, I'm giving it to her Sunday night." Mother told me that she wrapped it back-up and would have it here waiting when I come. I told her that I would be right over. I had already had my shower so I put on my attire and headed out the door.

I pulled up to the nosey people tower that mom lives in and as soon as I got out of the car, I heard somebody say "aren't you Ms. Martha's boy?" I said "yea, her son, who's asking?" One ole man in a hover round said this Tommy from upstairs you got a cigarette? I said "man I don't smoke" and walked in and rang the buzzer. After waiting a few minutes I rang the buzzer again and still no answer. I called mama's phone and she didn't pick up. Now I'm getting nervous so I can see in the lobby and the elevator opens and there is mom with Mr. Oscar holding hands and giggling and shit. She saw me and came over and opened the door. I said "I've been out here for about 5 mins ma," she said "oh well did you die?" Then she and Mr. Oscar busted out laughing as we all walked to her apartment. As we went in, Mom went to her bedroom, Oscar went to the refrigerator and grabbed a beer and I went into the living room. I see things between these two are pretty serious. I sat down on the love seat and mom said "move to the chair son." I got up and looked at her real funny, she said "come on Os." They both sit on the love seat together like that's their spot. I just shook my head and kind of smirked at the thought of my mom being in love all over again. I asked "mom why didn't you have your cell on you?" She said "cause I'm grown and I do what I want to do." "Really mom," I asked? She looked at Oscar and said "what? Was I being smart?" Oscar just looked up in the air and said "I'm not in it." I said, "Mom everything is not a Joke. I'm just asking because I was worried because you didn't answer." Mom answered, "Oh boy I'm fine. I just forgot it when I walked up to Oscar's house with him. Sometimes we just have our minds on other things and then she coughed and cut her eye over to him." I jumped up and said, "Okay mom TMI, thanks for the box I will call you tomorrow love ya bye!" I walked to the door and mom followed saying "whatever you do on Sunday night be sincere and open your heart for a new beginning. You will be fine son, go get that woman." Mom grabbed me by my wrist and kissed my cheek, telling me to "have a great night son. I can't wait to meet my soon to be daughter in law." I said "mom how would you know if that's what she will become?" Mom said "it's the twinkle in your eye and all those pretty white teeth showing only a princess can make my prince glow like that, now get on and call me tomorrow." I said "I will mom" as I walked out with my heart racing and my mind moving faster than a speeding bullet. Once in the lobby there was a woman looking at me and pinching her nipple, I took that time and listened to my brain when it said RUN!!!

Chapter 23

MO'NAE

Since I woke up this morning, this whole day has been moving very fast. I should have got up and went to church because I plan on sinning tonight. I guess it's because of this special night I have planned for Calvin. I have been making sure to check things off my list as they happen. House is clean, candles lit, Groceries shopping done, Hair tight, and Dress ready.

Now that it's about noon, I will start dinner since he will be here at 4. I decided to fry some chicken and dip it in my famous homemade BBQ sauce then bake it for about 15 minutes for a better season. I made smashed garlic potatoes and fresh spinach, and I also have pasta salad in case he wants something cold. I wanted to show off with my cheesecake from scratch. I have my strawberries cut up for a topping and the whip cream on the side, to use on him. In the fridge I have soda, beer, and wine and on the bar everything he needs just in case he needs something stronger. I'm trying to make sure I remember everything he needs so that way he doesn't have a reason to leave. I even told him to bring a pair of PJ's because tonight was going to be long and he had to stay. I wanted him to feel right at home, I plan on fucking, feeding and sucking him so good that he will not want to leave ever.

I'm a little nervous because I know what I want to happen tonight, and that he is the one I want it to happen with. I couldn't ask for a better man the way he holds me, his kiss, and the words he says don't get more real than this. I'm so anxious just to know where this goes after tonight. No interruption at all, oh this must be him calling me now.

I pick up my phone and here we go; the number that ends in 6969, The Voice is on the phone. I say "hello," "he says my dick is so hard it hurts. I can not take it any more, I need to be inside of you like yesterday."

"Hey," I tried to say something.

He said, "No I need you, please let me enter inside of you again and grow inside as a banana to the peel."

I said in a low soft voice, "I can't, I don't know you. Besides that was a mistake, I didn't leave the door open on purpose."

The voice said to me "A mistake? but you created me, your body, your mind, thoughts, and your pheromones have triggered a response from my manhood and my tongue. It is me that you need, let me be the Doctor that gives you your lifetime examination from here on out. I know that deep in your soul you want this, that's why you told me that it was mine. I am only here for the pleasure of you. Allow me to give you what you want again and again. I don't want to go away, Please don't make me."

I didn't know what to say because I did want all of this to happen. I just wasn't expecting it so soon, it caught me off gaurd. I say to him "but what happens if I do want you to go away? Wow, maybe I'm tripping."

"The voice then said no baby you ain't had this type of trip yet. You can't give a man a great drug and then expect him to go to rehab the next day. I have an addiction and it's you. See you soon" and he hung up the phone.

I needed to be slapped, what in the hell was I thinking, am I that damn insane to say something like that to a complete stranger. It doesn't matter what he says, when it's time to go he has to go. I'm over here waiting for the man of my dreams to walk through the door right now but have opened up a door to a whole different world. Again am I deranged? Is this man just made up in my mind or is he who I really need? Calvin has my heart, the voice has my body and is controlling it with his voice. Why am I so frail for this man that I don't know. Maybe the stroke of his tongue has power over me and only he can remove it, Or maybe because he put it on me so good that late night /early morning I need the job to be complete. Yes I think that's it. Finish me!!!

Chapter 24

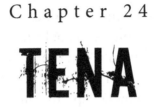

I have had so many different things happening until I just needed a little me time. So I decided to get out a little tonight. I wanted to call Monae for a girls night out but I Remembered she is preparing for a special night with her new man and plus she promised that she could get out with me next Saturday night.

Fuck it, I'm cool with being by myself this way I can clear my mind a little and enjoy something different. I grabbed my phone and scheduled a ride from Uber because I know I'm going to have more than a few drinks and I don't feel like driving anywhere. Right before leaving the house, I fixed myself a Jack Daniels mixed with Dr. Pepper just to help my nerves settle a little. I hate that I really don't have anyone to kick it with other than Monae, but like momma used to say Born by yourself, play by yourself.

This technology shit is crazy sitting here watching an app showing me where the driver is but so cool at the same time. The Uber driver pulled up in a nice BMW X6 so I got my strut on and I walked down the driveway to the car. I opened the door and got in as soon as I strapped my seat belt on, the driver started saying "TENA" the 1992 Prom Queen at North Roberson High! I could not believe my eyes. It was one of my so-called boyfriends named Larry. "Damn" I say to him "Larry you cute as fuck." He used to be torn up back in school, teeth were on Dynamite and he had a curl that didn't quite curl. I said "what's up Larry how are you?" He said "better now that I see you. Damn Tena Where have you been all these years?" I told him "just trying to survive Larry you know what I mean?" He said "yes so what are you doing catching an Uber, living in that Mansion?" I said "Nothing just wanted to get out without all that extra stuff. Besides, I want to be low key tonight, not seeking any kind of attention and I'm on my way to Thirsty Turtle to watch random people try their skills at karaoke. I heard this is a cool little spot to chill, just trying something different away from everybody I know." Larry said "yea I've been a few times myself, I really like it." We did some small talk till we got there, once he pulled up I told him hopefully I would see him again and to take care. Larry said "sure you will, take care and have fun." I tipped Larry and I walked in the place.

It was a few people sitting and chatting, some eating, others drinking. I waited to be seated and the young waitress told me I was able to sit anywhere I wanted. I chose the first seat closest to the door where I can see who comes in and out, New place can't trust anybody. Once seated, I looked at the menu, and another young waitress who stated her name as Callie asked me what I would like to drink. I asked her what a Redneck Fish Bowl was? She said "it was a very large drink with moonshine and other liquor in it; you can get it in different colors." I ordered a Red one and asked if I could go ahead and order some lemon pepper wings, flats only. Callie said "sure" and went to get my order. Sitting here waiting I jumped on my phone to see what's going on with social media. I'm just strolling through my phone and I hear, "you want some company?" I looked up and it was Larry, I said "I thought you were somewhere still driving." He said "no I wanted to chill for a minute because tonight is very slow, if it's cool with you?" I said "go ahead and have a seat. I'm by myself anyways company would be pretty cool right now". Larry sat down and just started going all the way back reminiscing about school and our little crush on each other. We were laughing thinking about some of the stupid things we did back then. Callie came back and asked Larry for his order, which was a Bud Light and Hot wings with fries.

Then the music started and out came a man singing an old Michael Jackson song, we were jamming to it. This guy sounds pretty good.

Larry and I really enjoyed ourselves. I asked him since he was here with me did I have to schedule an Uber. He said "of course not. I've been looking for you for a while now." I said "yea whatever." He said "I really have Tena, you are the only girl I really ever had a connection with." I said while laughing, "Larry you are so full of it." Larry told me that after he lost his College sweetheart on the street almost two years ago, he decided to be solo until he could find the right one. I said "what do you mean to the streets?" Larry said that his ex-Marlana got on drugs so bad that he could not continue to let her take him down with her so he had to let her go. He went on to say how she was even the dope man's bitch. I said "I'm so sorry you had to go through that." Larry said "it's not your place to say sorry you didn't do anything." I said "I know but that's still so heartbreaking to hear." Larry said "I've moved past that now, I hope she's happy with her boy Carlos!" "Wait a minute" I said, "who did you just say?" Larry said "his name is Carlos and they meet every Thursday night at Motel 6 on Trinity Lane in East Nashville." All I could do was look at him with my mouth wide open. Then I said "Yes, I know a Big time drug dealer named Carlos. He used to sell dope to my ex." I had to go alone with this information because this is exactly what I need so I can fuck Carlos up. I asked Larry "how do you know this?" Larry said "because every Thursday I would go just so I can see if she is still doing drugs." Larry also stated that his ex would hang out by the hotel until Carlos would arrive. I just could not believe this shit, he just proposed to me a few nights ago and now I have to hear this shit. Before I jump to any conclusions I need to see this for myself. I asked Larry if he would pick me up this Thursday so we could ride just to get his mind off her. He said "sure that would be nice and then was like are you asking me out on a date Tena?" I said "no Larry I just want to help a friend who is dealing with a heartbreak." Larry said "that he would come pick me up around 6 Thursday night". I asked if he could come around 8, I didn't tell Larry that's usually what time Carlos is gone. Larry took me home and told me it was nice to see me and I agreed.

Telena D.

I asked for his number and told him I would see him later then got out of the car. Talking about a mad bitch I'm steaming but have to control myself until then. I look up in the sky before walking in my house and ask God for strength for these days to come.

Chapter 25

Well the day is finally here and I get to go be with my queen. Monae told me to bring my PJ's, I don't feel like I'm going to need them, but I went ahead and grabbed them anyway, oh yea and the jewelry box. I am going to slip it on her neck when she is least expecting it. I can honestly say that tonight will be all about her and me. Not the Voice or anybody else she may fantasize about. I feel like the closer I get to my car the harder my dick gets because she is in for a real treat tonight. I'm aiming for the spot that made her say the pussy was his.

As I pull into the garage at her apartment for some reason now I'm the one a little jittery. Worried about If I don't make her feel better than him tonight, then I'm done as Calvin and will always give her him. Okay, now I'm jumping out the car with my overnight man bag, or hoe bag whatever people call it. I called Monae letting her know that I was about to get on the elevator, headed up to her. She answered the phone, sounding so electrifying. I guess once I plug into that spark, we will cause a major fire. I got up to her floor and rang the doorbell.

Monae opened the door, standing there looking stunning and good enough to sop up. Her black dress showed the swerve in all her curves. I had to have an inter talk with my man hood to not stand at attention as I gazed at her beauty. Monae asked if I was going to come in or just stand there staring at her. I have to admit I was lost for a second. I said" yes I'm coming in" and stepped into the romantic set apartment. Monae told me to sit my bag down anywhere I wanted too, then came over and gave me one of her passionate kisses. I wanted to take her right there, so I did what any man would do that's in competition with himself. I picked Monae up and kissed her deep and hard. I put her up on the wall and tore her panties off. At first I thought she would stop me but the more I did the more she wanted. I grabbed her by the ass and made her put her legs around my waist. I pulled my pants halfway down and rubbed the tip of my dick back and forward on her clit until the pussy was wet enough to enter. She went wild on this dick bouncing up and down, squeezing my dick so tight. Then in just a few more strokes she yelled she was cumming. I grabbed her shoulders pulling her all the way down and just held the dick in place for her to cum all over. She shook hard and said "OH my this is the best dick ever." I said "and you can get this whenever you want it, this is just the beginning of a long night." I pulled my dick out and it was covered with her cream, I just had to taste it so I had her rub her fingers on the tip to get the cream and put her fingers in my mouth. Mmm, I like my dessert before and after a meal.

After I tasted her she kissed me and said she wanted a taste too. After the creamy kiss, I let her down slowly but had to hold her for a minute because she said her knees were weak. She told me that I just did something to her that she's been wanting forever. I told her I was glad I could help, because It was something that I've wanted to do to you ever since we've been going out. I asked if I could go ahead and clean up so we could eat. She said "yes go ahead," while following me to the bathroom. We got in there and she sat on the side of the tub watching me soap up my dick and the more she stared the more it grew. I told her "don't worry you're going to get it," she said "I can't wait to feel you in me again, I mean we can skip dinner and come back to that later." I said "well I need food because that's energy for me, and you are an energy drainer right now." She said "dang it's like that?" I said "yea it is, so what did you cook because it smells really good in here?" She walked over to the sink and pulled up her skirt and while washing her wet pussy she started to tell me very seductively about each item that she prepared in the kitchen. While describing the food she was using her body as a Map for a Full course meal. I told her that she was about to make me take her again and she liked it, saying shit like I dare ya. She bent over the tub showing her Fat pussy and I couldn't resist. I slid all up in her, she was screaming in ecstasy. I grabbed her hips and deep stroked her, I grabbed her around the back of her neck and said "Who's pussy is this now?" Monae said "what did you say?" I said "I asked you who's pussy is this?" She started squirting all over me and said "Shiiiit Calvin it's yours, it's all yours." I rammed in and out and everytime I pulled out her juices would splash all over me. I asked her "you want this nut" She said "put it deep daddy." I pushed the dick as far as I could get it, releasing my load all in her. She started to grind as I came and now I'm the one with weak knees. I was sweating and jerking so bad, I'm sure I looked special because this pussy is the antibiotic for this mind infection that I have. She has just blown my mind completely and the thought of her fucking anyone but me could be a serious issue. I pulled out to keep from passing out and I asked "girl what the fuck you just do to me?" She said "I gave you what you asked for." I said "what does that mean?" Monae looked at me, laughed while washing her hands and said I'll see you in the kitchen. I was stunned. She spoke as if she knows I'm the voice but again I say if she doesn't ask me I will not tell.

Chapter 26

After all that great Bathroom Fucking, we finally made it to the kitchen. I told Calvin to have a seat and I would fix his plate. Calvin said "oh no, you cooked for me so I'm fixing the plates. He went ahead and put our plates on the table and we finally sat to eat. I'm sitting here with a dress and no panties on and he's sitting eating with his PJ's on because I got his clothes good and wet. I told Calvin that I just can't believe the way we went at each other. He said "I can, it was long overdue." Which he was right but I know I have had that dick before. Is he playing a game with me, I really hope not but that dick is fye and I know good dick just doesn't happen like that. Back to Back the voice one week then a week later Calvin. Maybe I'm just paranoid again. I have to say the voice was good because it was unplanned. Calvin is the bomb too but hell when he first came in that wasn't planned either. Well at this moment it doesn't even matter because after we eat I'm giving him an hour and I want some more of that dick. Calvin asked "what's got you in deep thought over there?" I said "you and how you just made me feel, Calvin I have not squirted in over 5 years and you come alone and take over my body. Singing….. How did you get here?" using the lyrics from the song "Nobody Suppose to be here" by Deborah Cox. He said "you had to have wanted me here in order for me to come in. I can only do what you allow." *Damn that sounded so familiar, he fucking with my head, and it's cool, I think.*

We finished our food and Calvin told me how perfect it was and how he couldn't wait to get seconds. I told him you already had seconds in the bathroom. He said yes but I'm getting thirds on that one but right now I'm talking about the real food. We sat and talked for a while, then I got up to put our plates away. Calvin asked besides me what was for dessert? I told him I had Strawberry Cheesecake and whipped cream if he wanted that too. He asked if I wanted a piece and I told him yes a very small piece with a few strawberries but no whip cream. He brought over my plate and stood behind me. I asked "what he was doing" and he said "this" and put something over my head and around my neck. I grabbed the object and said "Calvin what is this?" Calvin said "go look in the mirror." I jumped up and ran to my bedroom to see what he had put around my neck. To my surprise it was a beautiful 1 ct Diamond Heart Pendant in 10k yellow gold.

I said "Calvin you shouldn't have." He replied "yes I should have, I knew when I saw it that it would be perfect for you. That's why I had you grab it for me the day you and your friend were out that way." I turned around and said "this is something you give to your woman." He said "well isn't that what you are, Mine?" I was at a loss for words because I didn't know it would move this quickly. I said "are you sure that's what you want? I can't play games with you and I take relationships seriously. I have rules and I tend to fall in love quickly. I love sex and I." Calvin stuck his tongue in my mouth and shut me up real fast. He says "tell me you don't want me, And I will leave and never come back." The whole time he said all this he continued to kiss me. The heat was already on full blast. I told him I did. He said "you do what? say it." I couldn't do anything but kiss him. While he guided me over to the bed, He repeated it saying "say it, You do What?" His voice became more demanding as he flipped me on my stomach. He unzipped my dress and pulled it off. He starts at my feet kissing and sucking my toes. He is acting out everything the Voice said but I'm not stopping him and still I don't say anything. I just lay there moaning and enjoying all that he is giving. He says "Oh okay so you don't play games, so what game are you playing now, Quiet Mouse?" Now he is sucking on my thighs and I'm about to burst with pleasure. He grabbed my ass and slowly opened me like a book and started to lick my ass so good. He said it again this time his voice got faint because he acted as if he didn't want to come up for air. I was so wet from him just licking my ass, so when his tongue got close to my pussy hole. I came so hard he could fill my ass hole throb. That's when he knew he had me because I opened up my mouth and said "I do want you. I want you to stay right here with me, please don't ever go." Calvin flipped me over and covered my pussy with his mouth and began to sip the juices from my pussy. He was moaning and told me how good I tasted and how he could eat it all night. After I had come in his mouth his tongue was too much to take so I asked for the dick. He politely got up and said "next time I lick your ass I'm bringing an oxygen tank because I want to stay down there for a long time." He went into the bathroom and came back shortly. I could smell the toothpaste from his breath and thought damn he went to brush his teeth and I got this pussy right here waiting for him. He came back, lifted my legs in the air and gave me the Beast. I was experiencing pleasure and pain because he had me wide open and I didnt have any control. It all belonged to him, I loved every inch of it and I pulled him closer to me and told him I was about to cum again. This time he started to kiss me as I was about to cum he told me damn baby you feel so good can I come with you. This was so intense I put my nails in his back and yelled I love it while coming on his dick. His body sank into mine as he came with me and said "yes Monae but I love you!" His words caught me at the right time because I said, "I love you too Calvin", as we lay and enjoyed the after effect of "NOW", the most powerful pleasure I've ever experienced in my life.

Chapter 27

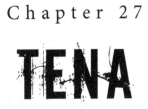

I'm in disbelief about this shit Larry just told me. I don't understand how Carlos could propose to me and have all these little Secrets on the side. When I ride out with Larry on thursday and I see for myself that he is fucking around on me I promise I am going to take all the money and run. I go ahead and turn on the shower so I can get ready for bed with a heated temp. I heard my cell ring and figured that it was Carlos calling, nope wrong it was Larry. I told him that he can not call me and it was not safe for him or me and besides I'm engaged. Larry told me that I left my wings from the Thirsty turtle in his car and I wanted him to return them. I said you can have him because I'm in no mood to eat at this moment. Larry quickly asked what was wrong, I told him everything is cool and would have to holla at him another time. Larry said okay and to call him anytime if I wanted to chat. I told him thanks and hung up. I went through my phone and deleted the Uber app. I erased Larry's name and hid his number as Monae's house number.

I can honestly say I cried because my heart felt a little different. I just can not understand how Carlos would make me feel like the luckiest girl in the world and then turn around and find out that he is cheating on me. I mean like why would Larry make up some bull shit like that? I really don't see why or maybe he is mad about losing the one he loves. Whatever the reason I feel crushed, I went ahead and got my shower and went to bed. I guess a few hours had passed because I was woken by Carlos rubbing my arm and down my legs asking me what's wrong? I asked him "why do you think something is wrong?" Carlos said "because you have dried tears on your face and while you were sleeping you sounded like you were crying." I told him that" everything was okay. I just feel my stomach cramping a little." Carlos believed me and asked, was there anything that he could do? I told him please get me some water and Tylenol and I should be okay. For the first time he actually acted as if he gave a damn and went and got me what I needed without hesitation. I took my meds and laid back down, Carlos laid down beside me and held me close while rubbing my back saying that everything will be okay. Even though I was mad as hell I still enjoyed being in his arms. The rubbing of his soft warm hands gave me comfort also knowing that at this moment he was my protector.

Morning came so quick so it seemed, I got up still so upset but I played it cool though. Carlos sat up in the bed and asked how I was feeling? I told him I felt much better than last night and that the Tylenol helped a lot. Carlos told me to get dressed. He had something special to show me. I can't lie I was a little excited because after everything he has done I'm sure this was going to be good. So for the moment I forgot about my heart ache and I came out with a cute little mini shirt and a tank top. Carlos said "baby do me a favor keep the tank top on, but put on a pair of your cute short shorts." I said "okay as you wish" and put on a pair of Golden Goose leather shorts. When I walked out Carlos was like, "Hell yea baby that Leather and that ass is perfect." I said "and it's all yours baby." He grabbed me by the hand and went out the kitchen door into the garage. Carlos had a Brand Spanking new 2020 Polaris Slingshot S. I was like "Dayyum, is this the Special thing you wanted to show me?" Carlos said "this is only part of it, now jump in, let's roll." I was very happy because I like to be out in the open. We headed out the garage and he stopped and realized he left his wallet in the house, he jumped out to go back in and I sat waiting. While he was in the house I noticed his phone was vibrating. I tried so hard not to look at it but the curiosity in me would not allow me to just sit there and look dumb. So I grabbed it and when I saw the hotel as the name I instantly got mad all over again. I was about to answer it when I heard the door close and the garage door coming down. I sat the phone back in its place and closed my eyes as if I was into the music that was playing. Carlos got in and was like he forgot he left the wallet in his pants from last night. He looked at me and said, ``Are you ready?" I said, "more than you will ever know.

Chapter 28

I left Monae's apartment around 1 p.m. dehydrated, weak and In love for sure. This woman put it on me, she even asked for some more before I walked out. I told her I was going to go to my place and get me a couple of hours of rest. Monae said that I could rest there. I told her no I couldn't because she was simply irresistible. It seemed like a long ass walk to the car and this bottle of water is just not enough to get my energy where it needs to be. I finally got in the car and turned my phone on. It went crazy with voicemails and text messages. Even then I was too tired to check them. I got home, called my mom and let her know I was okay and would call her back later. Of course she wanted details about if Monae liked her necklace and anything else I was willing to tell her. I said" mom I promise I will call you later and tell you about my night but not everything." She finally agreed to a call back and hung up. As soon as I hung up with her, my phone rang again. This time it is my angel, Monae. She called to see if I made it in. I told her yes and that I would talk to her later, she said okay and that she was about to get her a good nap in as well. We said our love lines and hung up.

I was sleeping so well when I heard the elevator buzzing as if someone wanted to come up. At first I just laid there then it started again. *I'm thinking who the fuck is this because noone comes here without asking me first. Matter of fact, who even knows I live here beside Monae?* Now I'm pissed because it's 6:50 and I was awake before I wanted to get up, when my alarm is set for 8pm. I go over to the Elevator and hit the speaker and ask "Who is it?" a soft voice says "Kim." I said "Kim who?" she answered "Kim from work, let me up?"

I said "naw hold on I'll be down there." So I grabbed my phone and saw that I had missed a few calls from Kim and was wondering what the hell she wanted. I only got about 5 hours of sleep and now the energy I just got back, I want to let Kim have it on an ass whooping for waking me up. I grabbed a pair of jeans and a T-Shirt and threw on my shoes and went down to the club.

There Kim was standing there looking kind of mad and sad at the same time. I asked her if she wanted something to drink. She said "yea a long island iced tea." I told my homie Darrin to hook her up as we sat down at one of the booths. I rushed her ass with questions. "What's up Kim? What are you doing here? I mean like how did you know where I live?" Kim said, "Calvin I know everything and I want to know how and when are you going to tell Monae about your little secret?" I looked around to see if anyone heard what she had said. I yelled for Darrin to come over and told him to bring me a Bud Lite. He walked away and I was like "look Kim why are you bringing this up now?" Without hesitation, Kim went in on me Saying "you can't be playing with Monae's heart like that. She is a good woman who deserves someone she can trust and I'm sure you haven't told her about the cameras and you being her stalker." I said, "Whoa, why out of all things would you care about that anyways. So I guess this is your way of trying to get back at me because she chose Dick over Pussy. Yea Kim I know you want her I can tell the way you look at her."

That made Kim infuriated, she said "okay Mister knows it all. I had her first!" I jumped up from the table and before I even realized I said "bitch you crazy now get the fuck out of my club. Darrin was on his way with the drinks and after witnessing this drama he turned around and said 'guess yall wont be needing these." Kim yelled at Darrin "yea bring me my drink cause I'm not going nowhere until Mr Lover Man hears everything I have to say." I told Darrin that we were going to go up to the apartment to finish our conversation, because customers were coming in and I didnt want my business out in the open. I grabbed Kim by her arm and said "let's go now." She followed behind because she had no other choice. I wouldn't let her arm go until we were in my apartment. Once the elevator opened to my apartment, I started yelling at her, pointing my finger in her face letting her know that this shit was foul that she was trying to do, and how things have changed since back then. Then I asked, "and what do you mean you had her first?"

Kim said "now if you will calm down I will explain everything to you." Kim sat there and told me way more than I wanted to even imagine. I told Kim "I cant deal with what you are saying, you mean to tell me that you and Monae had a weekend fuck session and I'm just suppose to believe it happened. Are you jealous because I didnt fuck you that night at Monae's party? So when you saw me put the camera in the bathroom you knew you could always have that over my head?"

Kim screamed at me saying, I never intended to blackmail you or anything of that nature. However I will not sit and watch you break her heart playing two different people in her life. I do have love for her and if you do not tell Monae the truth then I will.

The Elevator doors opened and there stood Monae saying "tell me what? And why the fuck are you here?", looking straight at Kim.

Chapter 29

I walked in and asked "what the fuck is going on in here?" Then I look straight at Calvin and say "so I'm the only female that's been here right? I came here to surprise you but looks like I'm the one that got surprised. I should have known you are just like the rest of these low down mutherfuckers.

"I turned to walk out and Calvin said "baby you got it wrong, I'm nothing like the others. Tell her Kim." Kim said "he's right because he is worse than the others."

Calvin yells at Kim telling her she wasn't shit and will make up anything to break us apart.

I told Calvin, "well it's working."

"Monae, please let me explain everything I promise to tell you the whole truth," Calvin said while looking at Kim. "Kim, you can stay to make sure I don't leave anything out."

I said "damn you Calvin, I can't believe you're messing with her too?"

Calvin rushed to correct me on that one saying, "Oh hell naw I aint never touched her ass."

Kim said "fuck you Calvin, now that part is the truth!"

I said "if somebody dont start telling me something I'm about to flip this bitch upside down."

With much attitude Kim said to Calvin, "You wanna go first or should I?"

Calvin spoke quickly and said "Monae I know this doesn't look good but Me and Kim have never messed around. To make a long story short, about a year and a half ago I came to your party. I'm sure you don't remember because you were really drunk. Kim invited me over and once I got there I knew I wanted you."

Kim tried to interrupt but Calvin told her that he has the floor and she can go after he is finished. Kim said "Whatever," rolling her eyes and all.

Calvin continued by saying "I knew Kim wanted to holla at me and that's why I came, but once I saw your beauty that's where all my interest went.

(Kim said "ain't this some shit" in a mumble.)

I watched you as you were sleeping on the couch, I asked Kim who you were and she told me everything that you've been through as long as she has known you. That's when I knew you needed a good man and decided to get to know you a little better for myself. I asked Kim if yall needed anything from the store because I was going to make a beer run. Kim told me more trash bags and a small bag of ice. So I went to Walmart and got the needed items and also a few other things." I said "like what?"

Kim laughed and said "Oh yea this is the good part."

I said "Kim."

She said "okay" and then gave me that look that she always gives in the office.

Calvin finished by saying "I got some mini cameras with night vision."

I stopped him right there and said" Oh my God you've been spying on me. I can't believe this fuck this I've heard enough."

Kim said, "Monae, please don't go until you know everything."

At this time I'm crying mad, looked over at Kim and said "this is what you've been trying to tell me?" In between my sniffles and crying pauses I said "Kim why didn't you just come out and tell me? I thought we were way better than this. I said ``I just can't do this right now" and I grabbed my purse and ran down the stairs because I didn't want to be in his place for another minute.

I got in my car and sat there until I could get myself together just so I could drive. When I noticed Kim and Calvin were outside and walking toward my car I took off squeeling tires. I was driving like a maniac, only to realize it was my life in danger. I calmed down, went to my apartment and packed some clothes. I called Hampton Inn & Suite in Smyrna so I can quarantine myself from the world for a few days.

Chapter 30

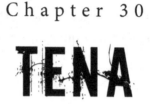

We headed toward the Huntsville Alabama exit, I asked Carlos "is this the surprise? A long ass ride to nowhere?" Carlos said "baby sit back and enjoy the ride." I told him" well turn the damn music up then." I guess we rode for about a couple of hours and then we got off the interstate. Carlos pulled over to the first Gas Station we saw so I could stretch my legs and grab something to drink. Once back in the car Carlos told me that when we do arrive at our destination, that I would have to put on a Blindfold before walking in. I asked "Why?" Carlos said "still part of the surprise sweetie." Another 10 mins down the road and he said well this is what I wanted to show you and turned onto another small street. I said "damn so this street is a surprise. WOW." He said "while you're trying to be smart this is a driveway not a street." I said "Oh my bad well it's as long as one." Then we pulled up at a Gate, Carlos buzzed then a computerized voice said "Please Enter Code." Carlos said, "Remember this Okay?" I said "Okay." He called out the numbers 0718. I put it in my phone in case he wanted me to tell him these numbers again. The gate opened and we drove up to What looked to be a Hotel hidden way back behind these trees. I jumped when my door was opened by a Big muscle Bound dude carrying an AR 15 on his side. I looked at Carlos and said "what is this all about?" That's when I realized that the place was filled with Men with guns. Carlos said "remember I need you to put on this blindfold like now" and handed It to me. I must admit I was scared as hell being surrounded by guns and blindfolded. Carlos came over to me and said I got you and grabbed me around the waist. I told him that I was not cool with being led blind into a place where I've never been. Carlos told me it's okay and to not panic. He told everything as we were doing it, like step up here, this is how many stairs were going up and he counted them as we walked up. I said how many more stairs with excitement. Carlos said just 3 more Tena I said okay cool. So we walked about 5 more seconds then Carlos said okay Now Turn to the left and stop.

Carlos told somebody to count to 3 and he would pull off the blindfold. 1...2...3 WELCOME HOME everyone shouted! I was appalled and elevated at the sametime. I looked at Carlos and said "HOME?" He said "yes baby, home." I looked over the balcony and all of his family was there, even Rico holding a baby, I damn near hit the floor. I asked Carlos How? I mean please explain? He said we are getting ready to talk about a lot of things. I waved at everyone and then was escorted down a hall to a room with double doors. Once in We walked over to the 12 person conference table. Carlos said we have so much to discuss and this is going to take a while. About that time N.J. and Chris walked in, Rico followed. Plus there were 3 Guards in the Large room with us.

Carlos sat at the head of the table close to the window, Rico sat at the other end close to the doors. I sat to the right side of Carlos, N.J. and Chris sat on the left side of the table and then Rico got and moved and sat on the other end on the right. One guard stood at the window and the other two stood at the doors. Carlos nodded to them and they opened the door and A woman with her head down walked in on a walker. I looked at Carlos like who is that. When she raised her head I stood up and said "Caroline you a " Caroline spoke and said" yes I'm alive and I'm sure you have a lot of questions?" I turned and looked at Carlos and asked "are you sure I need to be in this meeting?" Caroline spoke before Carlos could say anything and said "yes you are supposed to be here now please sit down so that we can explain everything to you.

I sat down and Carlos spoke first saying "N.J. Please give us all the information you have." N.J said "okay first Larry somehow found out about Tena being associated with the family and when she added the uber app he took the call."

I said "I don't understand what you're saying. Larry used to go to school with me and that's the first time I've seen him since. And how do you know about what app I downloaded?"

Carlos said "Tena I know all this sounds crazy but you have to listen to everything." I said "okay fine" and sat back to hear what was really happening. N.J also continued to say that the hidden tap on my phone confirms that he knows about the hotel and that he wanted to take Tena on Thursday to catch Marlana with Carlos. My inside connection said that Larry likes to ride solo because he doesn't like to share his findings.

Carlos said "that's what's up cuz, I appreciate that." Then Carlos says "Now Chris what you got man?" *I'm just sitting here really confused about what is going on.* Chris said "Larry has been Undercover for about 3 years. Marlana said that he started off as a ride alone about 5 years ago. He moved up quickly due to his dad being an officer for many years with Metro. Like N.J said For the information gathered he is working this case by himself and once he gets enough evidence he would call for backup. He is trying to use Tena as bait. That's all I have."

I'm sitting here with my mouth open like "What? using me as bait for what?"

Then Caroline begins to speak saying; "Tena I'm very sorry that noone has even told you why we are telling you any of this. First thing Welcome, this is all of our home, It's big enough where we don't have to see each other for days. Also each Family gets a wing so you and Carlos have the East wing which has 5 bedrooms 4 ½ baths, A Living Room, Kitchen and a bonus room. We feel that if we stay together then it's much easier to protect our own.

(*Thinking Well damn who put her in charge*)

Caroline continued "The real story to what is going on is I'm the Head over this whole drug trade."

(*My mouth dropped, did she just read my mind*)

"I know this is going to be a lot to take in but hear us out completely."

I said "okay I'm all ears."

Caroline said "the reason I had to disappear is because Larry was trying to set me up, he wanted to buy 10 keys from me and when I went to make the drop he and his boys pulled their guns out on me and my crew. Told me that he wanted everything and wasn't going to pay me a penny. My main Guard Big X jumped in front of me and pushed me to the ground. He got shot in his arm but the bullet went through him and hit me in my hip. My guys came through for me and got me out of there but a few people lost their lives that day. Larry has been seeking revenge ever since, so we had to lie to a lot of people about my death and we thought that he would leave us alone, Boy was we wrong. We kidnapped Marlana and found out that he was beating on her so we came up with a plan to help get her out by acting to be on drugs. She would steal the drugs he would take from small dealers and bring it to us. Trust me we pay her and take care of her and she helps me with the baby. So not only is he mad about not catching me he is also mad about Marlana and thinking she and Carlos are messing around.

She smiles and says "Oh yeah his name is Rico." I looked at Rico as if to say I know him. "No, not him. I'm talking about my baby, which we call him JR." Rico grabs Caroline's hand and kisses it. I said "Congrats" and cut my eyes back at Carlos. I wanted to slap everyone at the table for keeping me in the dark.

Caroline then says, "Tena Larry is a dangerous man that's why we are here. This is all of our home and we are all protected, however we need you to still be our bait, Carlos will explain this part to you."

Carlos asked me if I was okay. I told him "shit I'm not sure." He said "I'm so sorry baby but now that you know about everything. I have to let you know that was the real reason I put all the money in your name so in case if anything happens to me, you can get the money and invest in something legit. Baby in no way am I using you because money doesn't mean nothing to me I make too much of it.

I promise we are not hurting for anything and you can do whatever you want with that money after you do this one thing for me." I said "okay Carlos, what do you want me to do?" Carlos said "tomorrow I want you to go riding to the hotel with him. After about 10-15 minutes Marlana and I are going to walk out and I want you to jump out the car and go off on me. Marlana is going to act her part and lure him into the room. Once he walks in I need you and Marlana to run and get in the Black Escalade with Zeek he will bring you two back to the house."

I said "what about you Carlos what are you going to do?"

He said "don't worry about me, I will be back Friday morning."

I said "what about our house in Brentwood?"

He said "we don't have a house in Brentwood, I sold it a couple of weeks back. All of our stuff is on the way here so you will never have anything to worry about ever again."

Carlos looked around the table and asked, was there anything else we needed to discuss? Everyone shook their heads no and got up from the table. I was the only one still sitting in a daze. Carlos said "Baby you need to come on and let's get some sleep because tomorrow will be a long day." I told him that I'm sure it will be and that he better make sure I'm safe the whole entire time. Carlos said "only the best will be with me and to do only as he says." I said "okay it better be just like that" and I walked past him feeling used and dumb. All I really wanna do right now is get my money and leave, but because I'm a daredevil I can't wait to see how this shit goes down.

Chapter 31

I feel so defeated about this thing called love, maybe it's just not for me. Seems like once I open my heart, some fool always manages to deflate it. Since we are still off work due to the CoronaVirus I decided to stay here for a week just so I can get me and my thoughts together. Nobody can just pop up and I'm monitoring my calls for No Good People so I can reject those calls.

I got a little hungry earlier so I had Grub Hub to deliver me some Panda Express and after that I've just been laying around all day. I decided to go over to the corner store and get a few things. I grabbed a bottle of Cupcake Moscato d'asti, a fruit cup and a pack of AA Energizer batteries. I had to make sure my vibrating friend can last as long as I need it too. A couple of two liters of soda oh yea a pickle and a six pack of Mike's Hard Black Cherry coolers. I can say that I am content with my weird groceries of choice. I paid for it and headed to the car. When I got to the door to go out of the store, a well dressed dark piece of meat (I mean man) was holding the door for me. I looked at him and thought Damn and said "thank you" as sweetly as I could say it.

"Do you need help putting those bags in the car?"

I guess he asked because I was struggling with all this heavy shit. Me being me said "oh no I'm fine but thank you." As soon as I said that the bag that had the 2 soda's and my batteries, tore and my shit went rolling on the sidewalk.

He said "I got it" and picked my stuff up and carried it over to my car. He got to my car and said "Nice car, I guess great minds think alike" and pointed out that he had the same exact 2019 Mercedes Benz E-Class except his car was Black and mine was blue.

I said "yea It looks that way don't it. I really appreciate your hospitality because it's hard to find good people anywhere."

He said "you are more than welcome, what's your name?" I said "Monae and yours?"

"LaRon Harris you've probably seen my name on a commercial. I'm running for City Council in Chattanooga but then again maybe you haven't because everyone who sees me always recognizes me at first sight."

I told him "sorry Mr. City Council, I don't have time to watch T.V. I actually have a life and if you will excuse me I have to go but it was nice speaking with you and have a good day." I got in the car and he was just standing there watching me pull off. Shaking his head like okay and smiling as if he had just got dissed. I drove right across the street to the hotel and as I was getting out he yelled across to me, "Do you need help taking those soda's out?"

I said "yes why are you coming to help?" He yelled "yea hold on I'm on the way." He walked in the store and I went ahead and grabbed what I could to take into my room. Once I sat all the other stuff down I went out to grab the drinks and he pulled up and said "I thought you were going to let me get them for you?"

I said "well here you go, I guess I did get something free from the store." He said "did you just call me free?" I said "you are correct, you catch on real quick". *I guess my iced out heart is not letting me feel if this is right or wrong.* I'm letting this fine ass man in the room with me and I dont have a clue to what he might do or really who the fuck he is. I came straight out and asked, "Are you married?" He said yes, now does the answer help you with what your next move will be? I said "yes it does, now do you have a condom?" He pulled out a magnum and I pulled off my clothes. I said "Mr. City Counsel this is all I want." I unzipped his pants and he pulled them down. I pushed him back on the bed, slid that condom in a flash and straddled that dick like a horse. I rode it, rolled it, slid it, and surfed it. I let all my frustration about Calvin out on this strange dick. It wasn't as good as Calvin but It was a great ride and I'm sure it's perfect for somebody but for me it was just a piece of sausage to go with my scrambled eggs. I could tell he was fighting to make it last longer but I gripped that dick hard as I came for the second time and told him to let go. After he nutted, I told him "Thank you for your services and a great orgasm, but can you leave now."

He laughed and was like "damn you just use me?"

I said "yes you used me first."

He said "and how was that?"

I said "well technically you used my sodas as an excuse to get in my room, so we are even."

Laron asked if he could shower before he left and I said sure. There are extra towels in the bathroom. LaRon got up and went in to shower. I laid across the bed partially satisfied and thinking if this was really worth the hurt but could still use a little more. I decide to wait until he leaves then I'll bring out the Rabbit. After about 15 mins LaRon came out fully dressed he said "if you ever need me again, I'll be in town until sunday" and put his card down on the table.

I asked "where are you from?" He said, "I'm from here. I just live in Chattanooga at the moment, plus it's my mom's birthday and I have to drop my nephew off to my brother.

"Okay, well have a nice time here and a safe trip back home."

"Can I at least have a hug?" he asked.

I said "of course you can, if that makes you feel better. Please dont feel bad for this hit and run. I needed it to help me with this situation, I'm in."

LaRon held me and said "if the man that made you this mad is worth fighting for then fight. You feel and look too good to be here by yourself."

I said "oh well some battles you just have to let be. No retreat, no surrender!" LaRon walked out and said "No matter what, no regrets, take care." I closed the door and opened my bag so I could finish taking care of my needs. High Speed here I cum. Yes I'm so selfish at this moment I'm only thinking about Monae.

Chapter 32

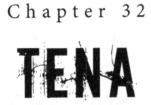

Larry pulled up at the Big empty house just a little early. I still ran out to the car as if I was so excited to see him. He hit the unlock button in the car and I jumped in and was like, "Hey, how have you been?'

"I'm good, beautiful, what about you?"

I'm trying so hard to come up with a story that sounds so real, so I decide on the half truth. So I say "Larry I have something to tell you. My life ain't as good as it looks. My boyfriend has been a drug dealer for a while. He has beaten my ass for no reason and I know he is cheating on me. When you and I had our convo last weekend, and you said the name Carlos. That's my boyfriend's name. Larry said "No way, are you serious?" *I looked at this Bitch like damn you're a better actor than me.* I continued with "That's why I wanted to ride to the hotel with you so I can see if it is him with your ex. He said, "Tena I'm so sorry I didn't know. We don't have to go tonight. I don't want to break up your relationship."

I said yes Larry Please go because I need to see this for myself. I just want the proof so I can get out now, before it's too late."

He pulled over in an alley. I said "what are we doing right here Larry?" He said "we have a few minutes before I usually see them and I just wanted to talk more about this before it's too late."

Scared because now that I know who I'm really with I had to play alone. I said "Larry since Carlos is so Big Time I want to catch him so I can leave with an excuse that's really it. Larry put his hand on my thigh and said "I'm sure it will be a great choice. Tena I can provide for you and we can start over with a life of our own. Now I don't have a lot of money in my savings but 30,000 should be enough to live nicely for a year until we get ourselves together."

I thought *Nigga 30,000 and I got over a million you must be a nut in a hut.*

I said "Larry that's a big move you would have to let me think about that one."

He said "okay but no too long I got something important coming up and I need to make it happen so you get 72 hours. That's when I'm pulling out."

"Larry um I'm not sure how you think I can make a decision in such a short time. I said I was going to leave Carlos but I didn't say that I was ready for that big of a change."

Larry looked at me and "said well I'm here for you" and leaned over to kiss me.

"Larry I can't." He said "yes you can '' and continued to try and kiss me. I told Larry to stop and he grabbed me by my neck and said No one tells me no. Larry said before we leave out this alley and before your heart gets broke by this no good ass nigga. You are going to give me some of that pussy no teasing this time like in school. *I started crying because this was not in the instructions given by Carlos or Caroline.* I said Larry, please don't do this. *Thinking now Carlos is supposed to have his guards on my trail. Where the fuck are they at now?* I started screaming as Larry forced himself on me telling me to take off my clothes. I saw he had his gun in his hand so I knew shit was real now.

So this crazy fucker basically going to rape me right here in this alley? Once I got my clothes off he sat his gun down on the floor board under his steering wheel. He spit on his hand and entered me as hard as he could. He held his hand over my mouth and was saying yeah that's what you get for doing me wrong in school. I couldn't say anything but take his small dick while I felt so mortified for even letting them put me in this dangerous setting.

Then I heard a loud pop and a liquid splashed all over me. I opened my eyes to see what just splashed in my face only to see Larry's head wide open with blood and Brains all over me. I started to scream when both doors on the car opened and it was Carlos and Big X. Carlos said "baby I got you you are safe now," and carried me to the Escalade that was parked behind Larry's car.

"Carlos I'm so sorry baby I didn't know he was going to do this." Carlos said "it's okay I knew something was up when yall didnt show up on time." He pulled out a bunch of towels and started to wipe me off. I just sat and cried while watching all the blood and meat that was covering my body. In shock I told him that my purse was in the car. Carlos said "don't worry everything will be taken care of. Oh yea and KaTena that will be the last man that will ever touch you, and I forgive you for All the things you have done. You understand what I'm saying right?" Still shaking I dropped my head and said "Yes Carlos." Carlos yells up to the driver and says, "Now Big X please take us home?"

Now I'm thinking *I really wonder what he means by All the things I've done. Does he mean ALL of it? And was that a threat? And he called me by my real name.*

Is this why he is moving me way out to the middle of nowhere?

Not knowing what he knows has me a little petrified.

Maybe he wanted Larry to killed me cause this nigga waited until that lil dick started poking me before he rescued me.

If it wasn't for all the money I got access to I would have been gone.

But hey call me the lucky one I didn't die, I got money and I live in the same house with all the dick I could ever want. If I can survive all this shit, it's meant for me to be on top. I'm going for the head now, Sweet Caroline, here I come!!

Chapter 33

MONAE

I have been here at this hotel for eight days now, I can honestly say that I am bored as shit. I've slept so long my body is sore, and the T.V. plays the same stuff over and over again. I see why people go crazy from not doing shit, or no one to talk to. This self quarantine is not so cool anymore and I need people in my life. After taking my phone off do not disturb mode I have a few voicemails that I'm not interested in listening too because I'm sure Calvin has a lot to say. As I scrolled through the calls I noticed only Kim and Calvin were the only missed calls. That seems odd because Tena usually calls by now. It's okay because I really needed a break from everything and everybody. So since I hadn't heard from her I tried calling but her phone was disconnected. That doesn't make any sense because she alway keeps her phone on or maybe she has had one of those crazy episodes that she has sometimes.

When you are the only person left in your family, you become dependent on no one but you. My adopted mother passed away sometime back and Being Adopted by a woman that was adopted I have not learned the importance of a Family yet. Well at least that's the way it seems for me. That's why I guess I always look for love in all the wrong places because in my life I have only had one person to really love me. It's hard to know what real love is. Crazy thing is I really do Love Calvin. I guess that's what love feels like. So is this the true meaning of Love hurts? Then I don't ever want to hurt again so I will keep my love to myself.

The sun had gone down and now I want some ice cream so I decided to go to Dairy Queen for one of their Strawberry Cheesecake Blizzard. Headed away from the hotel my phone started ringing. The number didn't look familiar to me but I went ahead and answered anyway. It had been a few days since I spoke to anyone on the phone. I said "hello."

"Hey girl this is Tena, I lost my phone and I had to move. I've been through so much shit and now I just need my friend to talk to me."

I said "girl you know exactly what to say because I need you too my friend." She told me about everything that happened to her and then I told her about everything that happened to me. We cried together then we laughed then we cried some more. This was the first time me and her had to go through something without the presence of the other. I ordered my blizzard and she was like "I wish I had a damn blizzard right now." I told her that when we hang out again we would catch up on all of the shopping and eating that we are needing in our life right now. I pulled back up at the hotel and finished talking to her while eating my blizzard. My car is still running but I have the lights off and I swear I just saw LaRon's car driving by slowly, or maybe I'm just turned on and wanted it to be. I told Tena about him and she said you slut and then like always she asked, "Was it good?" I told her well it was okay but not like Cal"…..my phone beeped. I looked and it was the 6969 number. I said "Tena I have to take this call but I will put your new number in my phone and call you back." Tena said "Okay sis I love you and I'm here for you if you need me." I told her "I love you more and the same goes here too."

I clicked over with the quickness and answered with my Important voice as if I didn't care who was calling but deep down between my legs all I could think about is the night he pleasured my mind and almost my soul. "Yea." I answered.

The voice said "sounds like you need some Sexual Healing."

"How would you know what I need?" (squeezing my thighs together tight)

"Because I'm your Doctor Feel Good and I know exactly what my patient needs."

"Okay, Dr. Feel Good tell me about it?"

"You are sexually ill and in need of more than a pill. Let me come to you and write you a prescription for stimulation. Leave the lights off so that I can use my xray vision to give you a full body examination."

I said "okay, this sounds familiar but you know what? you win. I'm giving you permission to come. I will leave the lights off for you. I'm in need of you to satisfy my everything, make me believe you are what I need. I'm at a hotel in Smyrna and I will text you the address and I will leave the room key behind the first bush wrapped up in a pair of my panties. I will be waiting" and this time I hung up.

Since he likes to play these games I am ready for the win. I rush and take a nice hot bath and straighten the room a little. I lit a candle in the bathroom so it's enough to see the outline of my full figured body. I turn on my slow jam playlist from Prime Music and lay on the bed waiting for the door to open.

I was so into the music and what was to come until I didnt hear the door open but I heard it close. I said "you didn't waste any time getting here did you?" I felt him sit on the bed, I was getting nervous and horny all at the same time. He whispered in my ear "No and I'm keeping the panties." I could smell his cologne and that is an extra turn on for me. He started at my neck and as he promised, gave me an examination with only his mouth. My deep breaths turned into oohh's and aahh's. My nipples became hard, I was soaking wet from his magic. He rubbed his soft hands between my thighs and all over my body. This time it was different and it felt more intimate. I was so aroused I wanted mind control. So I would think of things I wanted him to do like lick here, kiss right there and suck this and once all tasks were completed I would cum. He rubbed all around it as if he was playing with my mind. He knew I wanted him to operate on this painful throb. He began to lick the sides of my pussy causing me to gyrate my hips to try and catch his tongue on my clit. Because

I wanted it so bad I lost control and started to jerk from coming so hard. This man hadn't even fucked me yet and I'm losing.

I said to him "damn you real good I could get used to this.

He said "good" and got up off the bed.

I said "where are you?"

He turned on the light and said "I'm right here, now do you want me to finish or do you want me to leave?"

I was in total awe, "Calvin? OMG, how did you get here?'

"The same way I came at the beginning, your body called for me," he said.

"So this is the other part you were trying to tell me?"

Calvin said "yes now answer the question?"

I said "you can't leave, I need you here to finish what you started?" And just like that there we were fucking each others brains out. I know this is a crazy situation but I feel like I got my cake and now I'm eating it and It's so so dayum sweet!!!

Chapter 34

After we had sex over and over again, I think I apologized to Monae a thousand times. I told her I never intended for things to get out of hand but since Kim was in hater mode, I had no other choice but to come clean.

Monae said "You should have told me how you were feeling without all the extra stuff."

I said "I wanted to but watching you and knowing that my voice and me as Calvin was the only thing on your mind, was making me crazy but in a good way. Monae I would never do anything to hurt your heart intentionally. I was just caught up but the real word is in Love. I wanted you to be my woman a long time ago, and as you can see I was willing to do whatever to make it happen. I was in competition with myself. When you said that the pussy was his I got jealous."

Monae said "What, I don't know, I think you're crazy for real" she said while laughing.

I told her "I'm glad we can laugh about it because the night you found out the truth I cried."

Monae asked "are you for real?"

"Monae, Yes I was so hurt thinking that I just lost the best thing that ever came into my life. I was torn up and asked Kim if she witnessed it and told me how sorry she was for bringing everything up."

Monae asked "So how and why did you do the voice?"

I said, "I wanted to give you a Hellava fantasy so when you get hit with reality then you would know the difference and know that you can have the best of both worlds."

Monae said "Oh really?"

"Yes, I Aim to please and I love the role play and to see you play in that pussy. I can say I did that!"

She said "yea you did it and as crazy as it is I like it."

I kissed her and said "but I want you to love it." She laid back on the bed and said "I do love it and I love you and I love the way you and him make me feel. So could you make me feel that feeling again?" I told her "Yes Baby whatever your mind and Body desire I'm here to do it." For the first time since we've been together this is the first time we made love and it was well worth the wait.

Once we got finished with the last session we were really tired. Monae said, "Calvin, no more secrets ever."

I said, "the same goes for you Miss Lady."

Monae said "okay then well I got one."

I was like "go ahead." and I kinda got a little on the defensive side because I don't know what she is about to say.

"Well, I kinda have missed my period this month. I mean it could still come but I usually come at the beginning of the month and it's the end. More like a couple days late."

I jumped up with excitement, "Is it mine or the dude with the voice? no baby I'm just playing" with a big smile on my face.

She said, "I think it happened when you played him and came in unexpectedly."

"Well that means that you all too be glad it was me because we would be having some major issues right now. But when will you find out for sure?"

Monae said, "I will buy a test tomorrow and let you know then."

I said okay, are there any more secrets? I don't have any more."

Monae said "no more secrets, now let's go to sleep."

I kissed her and told her "Sweet dreams baby," she kissed me back and said "you too, I love you!" I told her "I love you more" and then pulled her naked body close to mine trying to be her cover and pillow so that she could have a Great restful and peaceful night.

Chapter 35

MONAE

Calvin helped me get all my stuff from the hotel and took it to my apartment. Once we got there he took out all the hidden cameras he had in my bathroom, bedroom and living room.

I told him "I just can't believe you were this obsessed with me, that you were willing to go through all of this just to secretly get to know me".

He dropped his head and said "I know this was horrible and I had no right to do this to you."

I said "you are so right and wrong at the same time. So tell me, was it something wrong with you for doing it or something wrong with me for forgiving you so easily?" He said "maybe it's both of us and that's why we are together because we were made weird just for each other." I looked at him and said "hmm good point."

Calvin said "I'm so glad we got all our secrets out because I couldn't live knowing that I've kept something from you after the fact that we have had our talk. Look, I gotta run to the house and pick up the present for my mother's birthday today. I want you to go and meet my family."

I said "I must be special. I get to meet the family."

Calvin kissed me and said I will be back in an hour to get you please be ready."

Once he was gone, I ran to the store real quick and bought a pregnancy test and was scared to look at it by myself. I called Tena so me and her can find out together.

"Hey Tena, what are you up to?"

"Not much just enjoying this Big Ass Mansion, sis you have got to come out here and see this shit you would not believe how big it is. Carlos bought me a Brand New Ranger to match his and I got a new wardrobe. Wait a minute holdup why the fuck you so quiet?"

Oh Tena I was only listening to you and how happy you seem. I'm really happy things are going well for you."

Tena then said "but bestie you sound like you got something on your mind. Let's talk."

"Okay Tena, the real reason I called is because........."

Tena said "because WHAT?"

"I just took a test"

"Oh no Mo'nae you got aids?"

I said "hell no, crazy ass girl."

"CoronaVirus?"

"No Tena a pregnancy test."

Tena let out a scream and started laughing real loud.

I said "Tena stop laughing I called you so we can find out together and you playing and shit. Never mind, I knew I shouldn't have called you. You never take anything serious. Everything is not a joke."

Tena said "I'm sorry bestie, so what's the result?"

"I don't know yet."

"What do you mean you don't know yet?

"Tena I took the test and I just thought that everything that we have been through lately, this is something that we could find out together. So let me call you on messenger so we can see this at the same time." Tena said "Okay" and hung up.

I called her back on messenger and she answered fast as hell. "Okay friend I said, I want to show you first before I look at it. Don't say anything until I look at it, Okay?"

Tena said "Okay let's do it?"

I picked up the test and said with a deep breath. "Here it goes." I pointed the camera toward the test and looked away. "Tena said stop shaking so I can see."

Before I looked at the test I turned the phone back so I could see Tena's expression. She just looked at me like nothing was wrong. So I let her see me look at the test. she saw my eyes light up and started saying "I'm gonna be a Godmother, YES!!

I got emotional as hell, Tena was like "It's okay why are you crying. I told her" Tena this could have been a very bad thing if Calvin had never come clean about him being the guy with the voice."

Tena said "well now you know and think about it, It's all good you know who's baby you are having. Now how are you going to tell him?"

"I'm about to get ready to go over to meet his family and now that I know for sure. I might as well tell him over there when I tell his mom Happy Birthday." We both started laughing and Tena said "I'm sure everyone will be happy, because I can't wait to start buying stuff," Well we have a ways to go for that Tena. But anyways I will let you know how it all goes, Love ya girl. Tena said ditto and we hung up.

After about an hour or so later Calvin called and said he would be pulling up in about 5 minutes. I told him that I would head down and see him soon. I'm not sure if I'm nervous or what but I ran to the bathroom and threw up nothing, Just a bunch of yellow liquid. I got myself together, brushed my teeth and grabbed some saltine crackers. I headed out the door and got in the elevator and I felt like I was about to get sick again. This has to be my nerves, going to meet his family and finding out I'm pregnant has got me shook up a little. I got to the car as always Calvin was waiting to open my door. He looked at me and asked if I was okay. I told him I'm good and got in. On our way to his mom he had me rolling talking about the woman who licks her tongue out at him and all about Mr. Oscar.

We pulled up in the parking lot and all the old people outside turned and stared at us until we got in the building. He pushed a button that had an apartment # on it and we were buzzed in. We had to sign a book with the time apt # and our name. We went in and Calvin introduced me to his mom. She was as sweet as ever, she looked me up and down, smiled and said `` welcome to our family" then winked her eyes. I told her who I was, she hugged me and said "I know, Calvin has told me everything about you. You can call me mom now so Come on in and have a seat." We walked into the small living room where a man was sitting smiling at me. Calvin said "this is Mr. Oscar." I spoke and sat down on the couch. Calvin went in the kitchen and told his mom Happy Birthday and handed her her gift. I said "Happy Birthday." After a while we were getting ready to eat and I heard Calvin ask his mom had she heard from Bruh. She said he was running late and would be here soon. We went ahead and ate and then sat and talked for a couple of hours. That's when I decided to say "I have something to say If It's okay?" Calvin and his mom told me to go ahead. "Well I took a Pregnancy test today and it came back Positive." Calvin jumped up with excitement and his mom said I knew you had a glow about you. I looked at her and she said "why do you think I said welcome to the family." By this time her door buzzer was going off. Calvin said he would get it while me and his mom continued to talk about the pregnancy, and how early I was able to find out. I heard a little boy say "Daddy." Then she got up and went into the kitchen. I heard "Hey baby how are you? The little boy said "I'm fine Gigi." Then Calvin was like "what's up bro?" The other manly voice says "What's up little bro?" There was a lot of laughing and chattering before I heard Calvin say "come and meet my Lady."

Calvin walked in with a little boy and said" Monae, this is CJ my son." I said well hello CJ aren't you handsome?" Calvin said "he got it from his daddy." I said "I see." CJ said thank you and smiled while half way hiding behind his dad. Then mom walked in and said "Monae I want you to meet My oldest son La'Ron." I looked up and instantly got sick and threw up right on the floor. Calvin came over to me and looked at his brother, "sorry about that man. She is pregnant." La'Ron looked like he had been hit in the face with hot water because his dark skin got really flushed. Calvin's mom told me to sit down and she handed me a wet washcloth. I said "sorry I got sick before I could shake your hand." LaRon said "no it's okay I understand, No regrets."

I told Calvin that I hate to have to run off but I really need to go home and lay down. Everyone understood and I told mom how much I enjoyed meeting her and couldn't wait to come back. She said anytime you want my soon to be daughter I looked at Laron, CJ and Mr Oscar and waved bye. Mr. Oscar said "hope you feel better young lady" I said "Thank you." LaRon tried to be kind of slick and say get plenty of rest and it was a pleasure meeting you and winked his eye. I gave him a half grin and walked out the apartment.

On our way back to my place I asked "Calvin where do we go from here?"

Calvin said "all the way up, we're gonna rock this thing called Love."

I said, "Sounds good to me."

About that time my phone rang and because the number was local I answered it. A familiar voice says. "I need to cum on that baby's head real soon, so my lil brother dont find out about us. I instantly got sick and threw up in Calvins car. Calvin grabbed my phone to save it from getting wet and I snatched it from him and threw it out the window. He asked if was I okay, and said who was that? I said they had the wrong number.

I laid my head back on the headrest with yellow acid and food all over my clothes and thought : *I know we said no secrets well this is one that will never get out. From the mouth of the Great Gerald Levert, "I'm taking this one to my grave."*

HEAVY BURDENS

Heavy Burdens, All night Cries
In need for a drink
To deal with the lies.
Why me? Why do you do the things you do,
Is this the love that you show your Boo?
Blacken Eye's, swollen lips, broken arms
Fractured hips.
Scared as hell because of the threats,
My mistake, your promise of breaking my neck.
Sleeping with one eye open, afraid of what you might do,
So here's my chance to get back at you.
I packed my bags and took the gun,
I went to your friend's house and had some fun.
His sex was good, so I wanted some more
Until I saw you in the door.
Damn why do I feel so weak, unable to speak, wrapped up in this
sheet, knowing that my ass was going to get beat.
BUT...
You fell to your knees and the hurt was in your eye,
As hard as I tried I just couldn't lie or cry.
I wanted to run real fast
But instead I stood there and laughed.
You wanted to know why,
Why was I fucking your friend like he was my guy.
Well, since you want to know why,

I fucked him because you gave me a black eye.
Since I'm on a roll let me throw you the ball
For every ass whooping I took from you,
I fucked them all.
Yo friend...for the eye
Yo daddy...for the lip
Yo brother...for the arm and
Yo uncle...for the hip.
Ass beating for no reason I go straight to the hood,
And fuck someone close to you to make me feel good.
Now get up off your knees and leave my job here is not yet done,
Revenge is a mutherfucker aint it?
THIS MOFO PULLED OUT Another GUN.............SHIT!

Domestic Violence is never okay. If you need immediate assistance you can call The National Domestic Hotline at 1-800-799-7233 or go to their website at TheHotline.org for online help!

Printed in the United States
by Baker & Taylor Publisher Services